SLAY MY LOVE

LEE COLGIN

CONTENTS

ACKNOWLEDGMENTS

To the best critique partner in the galaxy, Kat Silver. Keep an eye out for her debut novel—it's gonna be killer. To everyone who read this and added your feedback and suggestions on Scribophile, your help was invaluable. To Caitlin Taylor for the beta read. To M.A. Hinkle for the editing and Jenni Lea for the proofread. To LesCourt Author Services for setting me up with great editors and for all the help in getting this ready for publication. To Natasha Snow for the gorgeous cover. Thanks, y'all are the best!

Content/Trigger Warning: Abusive relationship involving physical and emotional abuse (not between the main characters)

CONFRONTATION

Franklin

This vampire was supposed to be different, or so Franklin had been told. He watched from a distance, silent and still. Tonight was for reconnaissance. The Scourge wanted this one alive.

The vampire sat alone on a city park bench, legs crossed, chin up, eyes forward, gazing at a series of baseball fields. They'd been there over an hour, the vampire and the hunter. Franklin had followed him from the business district. Too bad he couldn't kill this one. It would be simple with him just sitting there, an easy target. Franklin's muscles were tense—coiled and ready—but he waited.

Attempting to catch a vampire alive was dangerous. Information was key. What were this vampire's habits? His strengths and weaknesses? His age and, along with it, his abilities? Who did he hang out with and who did he avoid? Where did he go to hunt?

The vamp was not quite six feet tall. He moved with a feline swagger, a sway in his hips suggesting he'd be a loose and limber fighter, difficult to pin down. He had shoulder-length dark hair tucked behind his ears, revealing an oval face, prominent cheekbones, and a small snub nose. Tight-fitting clothes, mostly black, left nothing extra to grab onto in a struggle. Boots. Steel-toe? Franklin couldn't tell, and it didn't matter. If it came to a fight, he would worry about fangs hidden behind thin lips, capable of tearing flesh and paralyzing muscles.

The trick to slaying vampires was limiting close contact to the killing blow. The rules were simple: don't let them in striking range; don't look into their eyes; angle for an opening to pierce the heart or take the head. Silver could be useful, but you couldn't rely on it unless you're ready to die. The older ones could resist it, and even the young would risk burns to win a meal.

Watching the vampire begged the question: What was he doing? There weren't any other people, so he wasn't hunting. Unless waiting for someone to stumble upon him and offer up their neck was his idea of hunting. Stupid vampire.

Franklin's mind drifted back to that afternoon's briefing with his commander.

"The new one is different," Chief Darrow had said. "We think he's alive—as in not undead—and we need to know more. Tail him, Denhart. Get us some intel."

Franklin had stood at attention, ready for a new mission. "You mean…the legends are true? There are living ones?"

"We suspect so. This one has been seen at dawn and dusk, enduring more sunlight than should be possible. Put together a strategy for a live capture. I want that vamp in my labs. I expect your mission proposal within the month, Lieutenant. If approved, you'll lead the team. Understood?"

Adrenaline surged. Another team leader position would put him first in line for a promotion. "Yes, sir."

"Keep me informed on your progress."

"Right."

A living vampire in Bristol Springs, and the mission was going to Franklin. *Hot damn.*

Mythology told of a living strain of vampires dating back as far as the creatures themselves, but Franklin had never seen one. Theories speculated the species had begun this way—alive, but also demonic. If specimens remained, descended from those original vampires, the Scourge wanted them for their research. How did the curse come to require death before transition? And how then were the undead able to spread it to humans? Legend had no answers to these questions, but modern science might.

His leg was cramping. He readjusted, his eyes never straying from the target. Franklin itched to take him out, but with a promotion within reach, he'd bide his time. Hell, he'd stand there watching the goon for a solid month if he had to. Anything to lead the team that would bring this vamp in.

Franklin rolled his shoulders and willed his muscles to relax. There wasn't going to be a fight tonight. Instead, he settled in to wait for whatever the vampire would do next. Time slowed. He wondered what the vampire was thinking, staring off into the distance. Maybe this one wasn't all there. It wasn't uncommon for them to get loopy with age, the curse breaking down the human brain. Then again, if Chief Darrow was right, this one might not have been human at all.

The vampire stood, stretched his lithe limbs, and walked away. Franklin would follow at a distance. As he left his hiding place, the creature stopped. Franklin froze, exposed. Luckily, the vampire just bent over, gathered some trash from the ground, and threw it into a garbage bin.

That was odd. Vampires were a worthless plague on humanity; they didn't care about litter. Hell, humans didn't care about litter.

The vampire continued on his way, his slow easy steps simple to follow. Franklin tailed behind.

It was going to be a long month.

Gianni

Paranoia was real. Of course, being stalked had a way of solidifying the feeling. Technically, it wasn't paranoia if it was *actually* happening, right? It was definitely happening, all of last night and again tonight—a presence lurking in his wake. Gianni had expected being the new guy in town would come with challenges. He welcomed the extra attention, but the only interest he'd received thus far was mean-spirited teasing and this creepy human who looked like he'd stepped out of a Sears catalog.

The stalker was tall, muscular, and didn't blend into shadows nearly as well as he must have thought. His movements were stilted and cautious. He wore generic, blue-collar clothes a decade past their prime. Brown cargo work pants, a dark matching button-up shirt, unremarkable sturdy material—probably all Dickies. They would be rough to the touch, not soft like Gianni's cashmere sweater. The stalker would blend in better delivering packages, not following a vampire around until the wee hours of the morning.

He was a handsome man, but would look even better with a fresh haircut and modern wardrobe. Maybe a beard. As he was, Gianni could only describe him as frumpy. Beautiful broad shoulders like his shouldn't be hidden under a stiff poly-cotton blend the color of soggy oatmeal. The Scourge must have been letting anyone in these days.

Gianni let his footsteps echo off the pavement, easy in the heeled Paul Evans boots he wore. Surely by now the slayer realized Gianni knew he was there. What sort of game was he playing? Gianni could hear his footfalls; even the attempt at muffling them was obvious.

It was time for answers. Gianni rounded the next corner and blazed ahead. Then he doubled back on his path to come up alongside the man. At least now something exciting would happen. They'd fight, or the stalker would flee. Or even better, he'd have his first conversation with a vampire slayer. Risky, but not boring.

Playing casual, Gianni slipped into step next to him. The slayer startled, darted away, and drew a knife—probably silver. Predictable. Gianni kept his posture easy and open despite the slayer's fighting stance. He'd remain unthreatening as long as he could, draw this experience out. It was the only interesting thing that had happened since he'd arrived in Bristol Springs.

Gianni offered a half-smile in greeting. "Hello."

The slayer stared at him warily and raised the knife. He wasn't going to make this simple.

"You've been following me for hours. Last night, too."

Still no answer, but the man looked surprised.

"You thought I didn't notice?"

Apparently, the slayer assumed his attempt at stealth had worked. *Amusing.* The man stood on the edge of his toes, battle-ready, but also holding himself back. Why?

Gianni took a careful step forward and extended his hand. "I'm Gianni."

The man neither accepted the handshake nor offered a name, but he stood his ground when Gianni encroached on his space. They studied one another. This close, Gianni saw the slayer's wide green eyes, bright with alarm; he had not expected this confrontation. Gianni breathed in. He smelled good. Clean. Behind the soap, his natural scent was sweet, like ripe pears and honey. Static energy bounced between them. There could still be a fight. Gianni almost wanted it. He could take this slayer; he'd trained for it. But he found the man intriguing. He'd rather have information.

"Why are you following me?"

The slayer's eyes shifted up and to the right; he was

searching for a lie. Gianni waited, thrilled with the novelty of the situation, balanced on the edge of danger together.

"Where are you from?" the slayer asked, avoiding the question. His voice was a lovely deep baritone. It would be sexy in the bedroom.

"Couldn't come up with a good enough lie, huh?" Gianni set a hand on his hip, smirking.

"Not one you'd believe, no." The stiff muscles and tense body language only made Gianni relax more. This slayer wasn't here to fight. He didn't know why, but for now, they were safe from each other.

"I came here from Philly. And you?"

The slayer's eyes shifted. He was taking in their surroundings, perhaps looking for an escape? Again, no answer.

Gianni attempted to put him at ease. "I'm not going to bite you. I'm not even hungry. Besides, I'm watching my figure." He grinned. No response from the slayer, not even a flutter of expression. He would be a tough nut to crack. "You can answer the question."

The slayer tilted his head, a bit like a puppy. "I'm not going to."

"Then this conversation is going to be quite dull, and I'd had such hopes for us, Buffy."

The slayer's scowl deepened. "Buffy?"

"What am I supposed to call you if you won't tell me your name? I mean, really, it's a compliment. Buffy was the chosen one. The best of your kind."

"I don't care what you call me."

"Buffy it is, then."

"Why are you here?"

"You think asking questions is fair, though you refuse to answer them? I'll tell you why I'm here when you tell me your name."

Gianni took a risk and leaned further forward, betting this

slayer wouldn't attack him. The man dropped his gaze to Gianni's mouth. Gianni ran his tongue along his lips, careful not to reveal fangs. The man took a step back.

Interesting.

"Are you afraid of me?" Gianni asked.

"Afraid." The slayer's eyebrows lifted. "No…I'm baffled."

"Because you've never met a vampire this charming?"

"Sure, we'll go with that," the slayer deadpanned.

"Now, now, no need to get surly."

Gianni tried to catch his emerald gaze, but the slayer would not look directly into his eyes. So he was superstitious as well as mysterious. The silence stretched.

"Don't you have some slaying to do?" Gianni prompted.

The man narrowed his gaze, perhaps irritated at being called out. "Not tonight. Unfortunately."

"Oh, I see. They keep you on a tight leash, huh? Whoever gives your orders must be a drag. No doubt you'll have to report all of this." An idea formed in his mind. He shouldn't. But resisting temptation never came easy for Gianni. "Best give them something juicy."

Gianni darted in and grazed the slayer's cheek with his lips as he passed by, his tongue leaving a wet trail on the stubbled flesh. Without turning around, he added, "Give them my warm regards, will you, Buffy? It really was a pleasure to meet you."

Would the slayer relay that part to his supervisors, or would he leave it out? Everything about the man pointed to an uptight, rigid personality. It would kill him either way—to admit it or to turn in an incomplete report. Perhaps he'd leave the encounter out altogether, pretend he'd been successful with his stalking, his target never the wiser. Gianni would ask when next they spoke. He had a feeling he'd be seeing his stalker again. Whatever the man wanted, he hadn't gotten it.

Making certain he hadn't been followed, Gianni made for his suite at the Farthing. A group of young vampires spotted him, some of them hiding their snickers, others not bothering. It was no secret Gianni had fled from Philly to Bristol Springs out of embarrassment. News like that traveled fast, and if he'd thought to escape it by moving, he'd been mistaken.

"Out looking for the city sovereign? Any luck?" one of them said with a smirk. Gianni hadn't learned their names. There'd be no need. They weren't out to make friends. He wouldn't encourage them with an answer.

"You haven't heard?" another chimed in. "He's not looking for sovereigns anymore. Only a king will do for *Prince Gianni.*"

Gianni ignored them and kept walking.

The Farthing was a large underground complex running a full quarter of the span of the city above it, encompassing nearly fifty square miles and containing multiple levels. Most of the region's vampires lived somewhere in this complex. Gianni had taken a suite of rooms near the center, thinking it would be a good location to meet people. Near the exit would have been better since he spent all his time prowling the streets of Bristol Springs rather than face the mocking from his fellows.

Gianni entered his rooms, locked his door, and leaned against it with a breath of relief. It was too early to go to sleep, but he couldn't resist the pull of his bed. Sinking into its comfort, he curled around his favorite pillow and closed his eyes. It had been a long week of keeping his chin up and holding onto his dignity by a hangnail. News of his folly was sure to die down eventually. It had to. He couldn't possibly be this lonely forever.

2

FRENEMIES

Franklin

Franklin parked his car in the secure underground lot. The Scourge operated from a series of industrial buildings outside the city, one of several satellite branches in the United States. The main headquarters were located in Barcelona. Franklin had never seen any of the European offices, though he longed to. His father, General Denhart, insisted his duty was to stay in their own country and protect it.

"Exterminate the vampires here. Then you can run off to Spain," he'd said back when Franklin was younger and dreaming of castles. It wasn't meant to be encouraging.

Denhart Senior tolerated no interest of Franklin's outside the family business. Generations of Denhart men protected the public by slaying vampires and fighting demons. Franklin would too. He'd make his father proud if it killed him, and in this line of work, it might.

In the main building, called the Foundry for its resemblance to metal factories, Franklin waited his turn to report to Chief

Darrow. Around him were other hunters, also finished for the night and ready to report. He knew these officers but wasn't friendly with them. They were rivals for the same promotions. Better not to make friends.

Ahead of him was Hutch Wilson, also a lieutenant hoping to move up the ranks. He wore a broad grin on his face, probably eager to brag about his night's work. Franklin avoided eye contact. The captain behind him didn't.

"What are you dying to tell us, Hutch?" she asked.

"Got lucky tonight, boys. Found two young vamps out together. Blood drunk and stupid enough to let their guard down." Hutch feigned a killing blow with a grin. "They didn't even see it coming."

One hunter typically wouldn't go after two vampires without backup, but Hutch's recklessness wasn't surprising; he was ambitious, like Franklin.

If Franklin hadn't been assigned to Gianni, he probably would have been dispatched for cleanup. Thanks to the prissy vampire, he'd been spared.

"Nice," Captain Ash replied. She always encouraged lower-ranking officers. "What about you, Denhart? Any news?"

Franklin wasn't about to say what really happened. "Nothing exciting. Just tailing the new one. So far, not much to report."

"That must be a drag," said Hutch, "following one around, not allowed to kill it."

Franklin thought of Gianni's lips on his cheek, his arrogance. He'd expected Gianni to attack him, but instead he'd struck up a conversation. Muddied the waters. When he'd invaded Franklin's space, there was no sense of danger, no fight-or-flight response. Franklin had frozen and let the brief cheek kiss happen. It would have been easier if his assignment was to kill him. Gianni didn't seem like a monster.

Hutch was waiting for an answer. Franklin reluctantly spoke

up. "They want him for the labs. It'll be worth the wait for a live capture."

Chief Darrow's door opened. With a nod to the waiting group as they saluted, General Labat exited the office, her cadets following on her heels. Ash, Hutch, and Franklin made their way in to give reports. Darrow's office was large enough for a conference table but so cluttered the space felt small. Shelves of books lined the walls, what books didn't fit on the shelves lay in piles on the floor, and papers were strewn about. Franklin never liked coming here; the mess made him feel claustrophobic.

If Franklin left out most of what happened, none were the wiser. He couldn't possibly tell Darrow he'd let the vampire within striking range. That he'd spoken with him. That Gianni had been more inquisitive and less violent than he'd thought possible for a vampire. He confessed to being caught spying and said the vampire had simply fled.

"You were spotted?" Darrow leaned forward in his chair. "Is this vampire going to be too much for you?"

"It won't happen again. Everything is under control, sir." Franklin swallowed, contemplating his future in the long pause. He wanted to keep this case. A live capture was a rare opportunity. He couldn't fuck up.

"Be careful next time." Darrow's gruff voice filled the room, and his attention turned to Ash.

Phew. It was over. Franklin was lucky not to be taken off the assignment. Darrow could easily have passed it to Hutch. The thought made his blood boil.

Back in his barracks room, Franklin rolled his shoulders to release tension, then sat down at his personal computer and logged the night's field notes. These records were his alone, so he left nothing out, admitting his failure on the screen. The word *Buffy* glaring in front of him set his teeth on edge. No way would Franklin give the fiend his real name. Names held power, and Franklin would give away none. He needed a new plan to convince this vampire to trust him.

Franklin never thought he'd brainstorm ideas to get closer to a bloodsucker, but if that's what it took, he would do it. He'd underestimated Gianni and let him get the upper hand. It wouldn't happen twice.

If Franklin returned to the park bench and waited, would the vampire seek him out? Instead of tracking Gianni, he could wait to be found. If it didn't work, Franklin could go back to stalking, but he had a feeling about this vampire. Gianni wanted his attention. If the vampire wanted to be close, Franklin could do close.

Gianni

Rising before the other vampires had its advantages, especially if one wanted to slip away unnoticed. Gianni left the Farthing at dusk. Sunlight, too low in the sky to harm him, filtered long across the horizon, beautiful golds and oranges streaking over the tree line. Gianni admired the picture it painted on his way to the library. He needed something useful to do other than endless window shopping. The city library was open late every Thursday, so he went straight there to see about getting a card.

He could go to vampire-owned establishments, of course. Nightclubs and gaming dens catered to unsuspecting humans on the front end and vampires in their exclusive private rooms. The old Gianni would have made a beeline to these places, eager to establish his rank in the pecking order. But he had no energy left for society.

Books never laughed at him.

Getting the card was simple; choosing books was harder.

Only twelve books could be checked out at once, and because of the schedule, Gianni could only come to the library on Thursdays. He'd finish all of these before then, so he had to choose wisely.

Gianni carried his bag, heavy with new goodies, toward the city park, only to find the slayer seated on his bench, waiting.

Interesting.

They stared at one another. The man's expression betrayed his self-satisfaction. *So he thinks I'm predictable?* That wouldn't do. Gianni sauntered toward him, torn between irritation and delight. Time to turn on the charm.

"Buffy."

"Gianni."

"Are you planning on slaying me this evening?"

"Probably not."

"Then scoot over." Gianni flung himself next to the slayer in the center of the bench. The man startled and slid away. Gianni followed. He leaned his weight against the slayer's arm. For a moment he thought the slayer would flee, but the man only stiffened and remained in place. Gianni set his bag on the empty side and crossed his legs.

"So how'd it go?" Gianni asked.

"How'd what go?"

"Telling your boss about last night, of course." Gianni watched him closely. When color crept into the slayer's cheeks, he knew. "Oh. You didn't tell them? Naughty Buffy. Did you lie?"

"I couldn't exactly tell him you licked me," came the irritated response, along with some serious side-eye.

Gianni laughed. "It was a whim. You can relax. I'll restrain myself tonight. Besides, you taste like cheap aftershave."

The slayer ignored the barb. Gianni would have to try harder.

"What's in the bag?" Buffy asked.

"Books."

"Books?" The slayer's eyebrows lifted, skeptical.

"Heard of them? Bits of paper stuck together with words on the pages? Surely you've seen one."

"Why books?"

"To read, Buffy. Try to keep up." *This shouldn't be so fun.* "I got them from the library, where the books live. If you're still stalking me next week, you should come."

"Hey, you found me tonight, not the other way around."

"You were waiting for me," Gianni countered. "You came here hoping I'd show."

The slayer shrugged. Guilty.

Silence settled between them. The park was often empty at this hour, but across the baseball field, a man walked alone. They both watched and waited until he was out of sight and their bubble of privacy was restored.

"What's your name?"

"I'm not going to tell you my name."

"Why not?"

"I'm not stupid, you know. It's not safe. You'll use it in some bizarre vampire ritual."

Gianni's eyes went wide. He flashed a vibrant smile—wide enough to reveal fangs—and doubled over in laughter. "You are not serious right now! Really? You honestly think I want your name? For what, some spell? Oh my god, you're joking. Right? Tell me you're joking." The novelty of the big belly laugh was such a joy.

The slayer glared at him, emerald green eyes perfectly serious.

Gianni met his gaze and chortled. "There's no 'bizarre vampire ritual,' okay? I'm not going to chant your name into a fire or something. Is that really what they teach you people?"

"You don't think I'll believe you over them, do you?"

"Obviously not right away, but I'll admit that sounds appealing."

"Don't hold your breath."

"Why'd you join anyway? The Scourge, I mean. What an awful name."

"It's an ancient name." The slayer looked away. "I'm brethren. My father was a hunter, as was his father before him."

For the first time, Gianni wasn't sure what to say. "Was?"

"My father retired due to injury. He's still alive. My grandfather was killed in the line of duty before I was born. I never got to meet him, though everyone tells me I look like him."

This had been a poor choice in conversation topics. "I'm torn. I want to say I'm sorry, but it was him or the vampire, right? I mean, you can hardly blame us for fighting back. Still...I'm sorry for your loss."

The slayer said nothing. They sat together quietly. On impulse, Gianni reached over and took his hand, their palms pressed together. The slayer stayed perfectly still; he didn't curl his fingers around Gianni's, but he didn't pull away either.

For a moment, neither of them breathed.

Gianni felt the slayer's pulse racing under his fingertips. A glance at his face revealed heat in his cheeks.

"You're warm," the slayer said. "I thought you'd be cold."

"You're wrong about a lot of things, Buffy."

"Why are you holding my hand?"

"I'm trying to be friendly," was what he said aloud, but inside, he wasn't sure. He'd wanted to touch the slayer.

"Do you hold hands with your other friends?"

"I don't have other friends." Gianni let go, put his hand back in his lap, and cast his eyes forward, scanning the park.

"That can't be true. Someone like you? You must have loads of friends."

"You're wrong about that, too."

The slayer reclaimed Gianni's hand.

Gianni returned to The Farthing feeling lighter despite his heavy bag full of books. Intending to hole up in his suite and read—and by *read* he meant *think about the handsome slayer he'd spent half the night talking to.* Upon hearing a familiar and unwelcome voice calling from down the hall, he froze.

"Ah, there's my pretty little strumpet now."

No fucking way. There stood Oswald, staring Gianni down, a throng of admirers already gathered around him. He looked imperious, as usual, a familiar haughty expression on his face. Fine gaudy clothes were draped elegantly over his broad shoulders, black hair glistening. As if he didn't stand out enough, he wore shades of purple, eggplant over lavender. Probably bespoke.

Gianni clung to his books. "What are *you* doing here?"

"Now, now, pet. Is that any way to speak to your elder?"

The bastard blocked his way. Gianni would have to get past him to get to his rooms. "I came to Bristol Springs to get away from you."

"I missed you," Oswald crooned, breaking from his groupies and prowling forward.

Gianni stepped back. "I hate you."

The group surrounding them were eating this up. Gianni felt their eyes on him like cobwebs; he needed to wipe them off. He turned and dashed out the same way he'd come.

Out of the Farthing and back onto the streets, Oswald's laughter echoed behind him. *Let them laugh.* He'd wait them out. They'd all have to sleep before Gianni needed to be underground.

It wasn't fair. Oswald shouldn't have been able to follow him there. He was the sovereign of Philadelphia and had responsibilities. Making this trip on such short notice would have taken some serious finagling—Gianni had only been gone a week.

Oswald didn't miss him; that much was bullshit. He'd come to see for himself how low his paramour had fallen. He wanted to rub it in, bathe in Gianni's disgrace, roll around in it until he'd had his fill. Oswald's vanity wouldn't be satisfied until he'd left Gianni broken.

Again.

3

BACK TO THE BOOKS

Franklin

*V*ampires were supposed to be cold. Dead. Gianni's hand was flush with life. As they'd suspected, he was different. The Scourge would want the confirmation. How could he report to Darrow without telling him they'd been… holding hands? Now that he thought about it, maybe Darrow didn't need all the details.

Franklin wrestled with his thoughts. Gianni didn't fit into the box he'd labeled *vampire* and marked for the trash. Gianni had a witty sense of humor, even if Franklin was the butt of his jokes. But Franklin could relate to his air of prevailing loneliness.

Tonight he'd been kind, offering comfort. Friendship.

None of that mattered. Vampires were not to be trusted, and Franklin suspected the smooth-tongued Gianni lied a great deal. He wasn't getting to know this creature in any real sense, only the bits the vampire wanted to reveal.

Capturing him alive wouldn't be as hard as Darrow thought. If Franklin could get Gianni to trust him, the vampire would practically hand himself over. After that, Franklin could endure whatever remorse emerged. Gianni was a killer who needed to be extinguished; it was the right thing to do.

Franklin made no report to Darrow. There wasn't an update worth sharing, although he'd have to think of something to tell the chief eventually. Would Darrow support his plan? Would he even believe a hunter capable of winning a vampire's trust? Definitely not. He'd log the night's happenings in his own file, and that would be it. Already things were out of hand, impossible to explain.

The other hunters also had a quiet shift. After Hutch's double slaying the night before, vampires kept to the shadows, and the city streets were peaceful.

Rather than join the poker tournament springing up amongst bored cadets, Franklin made his way to the school rooms. Here future hunters learned their vocation, studied their prey, and received lessons from the Scourge's professors. Franklin had spent much of his youth in these rooms, striving to outperform classmates.

What he wanted now was source material, the old mythology books detailing vampires who were actually alive. Time to take a closer look at these legends, to find something they weren't taught in school. He needed an advantage over Gianni, anything useful when dealing with the cagey vampire.

Selecting two large volumes, he took a seat at a desk and settled in for a long morning of research.

Franklin patrolled in Gianni's favorite places but found no trace of the vampire. Every night for five nights he checked the shops along the business district, the streets suspected of bearing entrances to the vampires' underground lair, the neighborhood around the library, and the city park Gianni frequented. Nothing. Darrow was becoming frustrated, and Franklin would need something to report soon.

Where was Gianni? Was the vampire avoiding him? Did he leave town, and Franklin's searches were all for naught? There was no way of knowing. He couldn't just walk up to another vamp and ask. Hunters and vampires didn't have conversations. Except for Franklin and Gianni. If he didn't find the vampire, Franklin would be reassigned, the opportunity lost. The possibility invaded his thoughts like a weed, tenacious in its persistence.

On the sixth night, Franklin rounded the corner by the ball-fields—and there he sat, posed primly on their bench, already waving at him. Franklin smiled without thinking, then banished the expression.

As Franklin approached, the vampire rose. The hunter stopped in his tracks. Gianni was stunning. His dark hair was done up in curls. Was he wearing makeup? Yes, he definitely had on makeup: eyes outlined in black, darkened lips, color in his cheeks. Was that rouge, or was he blushing? Franklin couldn't tell. Gianni wore white this evening, a stark contrast to the blacks he seemed to favor and striking next to his porcelain skin. Fabric flowed from delicate shoulders to slim hips. Feminine. The heels on his shoes made him nearly as tall as Franklin.

Franklin's gaze traveled from the vampire's feet to his face. Gianni looked delighted with the attention. He smirked, crossing his arms over his chest, and spoke.

"You're late."

"You look nice." It came out of Franklin's mouth unbidden. *What the hell?*

"You're forgiven." Gianni smiled and reached for him. Franklin came to his senses and stepped back, out of reach. Gianni's eyebrows lifted. "Jumpy tonight? I won't hurt you."

"Where have you been?"

"Why? Did you miss me?"

"I was worried."

Gianni smiled. This one seemed genuine. "Were you really?"

Franklin didn't know what to say. Was he worried? Yes. Should he have admitted it? Probably not. Things never went as planned around this infernal creature.

"It's been a rough week." Gianni let him off the hook. "It's good to see you."

Franklin went over a litany of responses in his head. *It's good to see you too. I've also had a rough week. Are you okay?* All were true. All he vetoed. Gianni made him tongue-tied. Fortunately, the vampire talked enough for both of them.

"My ex is in town. It would seem I have two stalkers. Lucky me. How about you? How goes the slaying?"

"Oh, um. It doesn't. I mean, I'm not patrolling right now."

"No. You were searching for me. Why?"

Franklin shrugged. Gianni was his assignment, but it wasn't as if he could say it, though surely the vampire was clever enough to have made that deduction. "You're interesting," was all he came up with.

"Am I? Sweet of you to notice." Gianni peered up at him through painted lashes. "So why is it you're not trying to slay me, exactly? Not that I'm complaining. I don't want to fight you."

Franklin was accustomed to straight answers. Could he tell Gianni the truth? The vampire would see through any lie he came up with on the spot. "I haven't been ordered to kill you."

An eyebrow lifted. "What have you been ordered to do?"

Franklin took a breath. "Monitor you."

"Why?"

Franklin was nearing his limit of safe topics. "The Scourge think you're different."

Gianni nodded, still staring at him through half-lidded eyes.

It was distracting. Franklin avoided his gaze. He needed something he could report back to Darrow. Something besides *the vampire is flirting with me.* And he needed to get them off this line of questioning.

"Your ex is stalking you? Is she powerful? Are you in danger?"

"He," Gianni corrected. Franklin supposed he knew that, but the *she* had slid off his tongue anyway. "One could argue a vampire hanging out with a vampire slayer is on the dangerous side, but no, I'm not in danger. He can't hurt me. We do have laws, Buffy."

"People break laws."

"They do. Still, he doesn't want to hurt me…well, not physically, not much."

"Not much?"

"Let's not talk about this." Gianni reached out again. This time Franklin let him approach. Gianni grazed his fingertips over Franklin's elbow. A casual touch, but Franklin felt it to his core, electric. "What about you. How've you been?"

Frustrated. Annoyed. Worried. "Fine."

"That's it, *fine?*"

"Maybe a little bored. No one snipes at me when you're not around. Where did you go?"

"Nowhere, just lying low. I can't be your only entertainment, Buffy. You need a hobby. One that doesn't involve killing. How about knitting? You could make me a sweater."

Franklin laughed. "I doubt you'd wear any sweater I was capable of making."

Gianni scrunched his nose.

Franklin tried to ignore how cute it was.

"You're probably right. A scarf, then? That should be simple enough." Gianni was looking past Franklin's shoulder. His eyes grew wide with alarm, and panic overtook the soft, teasing expression. "Shit. You have to go, Buffy, now!"

"What? Why?" Franklin turned to see a man approaching in

the distance. Too far away to tell if he was human or vampire, but Gianni's reaction indicated the latter.

Gianni's hands were on his shoulders, pushing him away. "I'll explain later, I promise. Don't try and watch either—he'll know. He'll kill you. Go! Meet me at the library tomorrow."

Panic didn't suit Gianni, and Franklin didn't like seeing it harden his soft features. "Will you be okay?"

"For fuck's sake, yes. Now go!" Gianni physically shoved him. Franklin reluctantly went with it, jogging away, still confused.

Looking for a place in the shadows where he could hide and eavesdrop was tempting, but something in Gianni's reaction warned him off. Was this the ex-boyfriend arriving? Was he an elder or particularly powerful somehow? Against every fiber in his being, Franklin trusted Gianni and hurried back to the safety of the Foundry, hoping Gianni was right when he said he'd be okay. These sudden protective feelings were unsettling. He brushed them aside. He'd meet Gianni at the library tomorrow and ask about it then. For now, he would do his best not to worry over a vampire.

Gianni

Relieved to see the slayer leave, Gianni turned his attention to the approaching asshole. The last thing he needed was Oswald seeing him casually chatting up a slayer.

Damn Oswald. He'd been having a nice time with Buffy. As the sovereign approached with a haughty swagger, Gianni had to admit Oswald filled out the blue pinstripe suit nicely, complementing his black hair hanging loose around his shoulders. Good looks wouldn't stop Gianni from hating him.

Oswald invaded Gianni's space, forcing him to either hold

his ground and be uncomfortably close or to back up. Gianni backed up.

"You've been avoiding me."

Gianni had been avoiding everyone. "No shit. How could you tell?"

Oswald made a clicking sound in the back of his throat. "Don't be rude. It doesn't suit you. You look nice." The words were said with a leer Gianni didn't care for. They'd sounded better coming from the slayer, more genuine.

"What are you doing here? You chased off my dinner."

"*You* chased off your dinner rather than share him with me. But not to worry. I'll take you hunting." Oswald crept forward.

Gianni took another step back. "You need to go."

"Come with me." Oswald reached for him.

Gianni slapped his hand aside. "No fucking way."

"Fucking would be nice right now. How about it? I know you miss this cock." Oswald gave himself a squeeze. Gianni should have expected this. The asshole couldn't handle being told no.

"Why are you here?"

"To bring you home. There's nothing for you but me. The sooner you realize it, the easier it will be for you."

"I'm done with you. The sooner *you* realize, the easier it will be for you."

Quick as lightning and far meaner, Oswald grabbed a handful of Gianni's curls and twisted, wrenching his neck sideways. Gianni yelped and struggled but couldn't free himself. Oswald shook him, and Gianni's brain rattled in his skull. His hands grasped at Oswald's, trying in vain to free himself.

Oswald drew him close, cool breath ghosting over his ear. "Be still. I've had enough of your lip. You're mine until I say otherwise." Oswald's teeth sunk into the flesh at Gianni's neck without warning. Gianni opened his mouth to scream, but no sound would come. The bite was vicious and brutally cruel, tearing his skin and bruising his muscles. Trembling, Gianni pushed against Oswald's chest to no avail. Pain bright and bursting blotted out his senses; Gianni closed his eyes and saw only red.

When the brute had taken all he wanted, he released Gianni with a shove, sending him sprawling. Gianni pressed his hand against the wound, holding it tight, but blood continued to flow freely.

Oswald slipped a gold handkerchief from his pocket and cleaned his mouth. He peered down at Gianni. "Oh, that looks bad, my dear. Would you like some help?" A sardonic grin revealed fangs still covered in Gianni's blood.

Gianni had to get Oswald to close the wound; it would not heal on its own, and he could bleed out from a bite of this magnitude. He didn't have the healing powers of other vampires, not yet. He hadn't thought Oswald would really hurt him. Surely the sovereign wouldn't risk letting him die. That was a capital offense.

"Just close it and get this over with," Gianni spat, staring at the ground.

"Say please."

"I could report this."

"But you won't. Say please, Gianni, or you'll regret it."

Gianni's head spun. His new shirt was soaked in his own blood. His vision blurred, so he closed his eyes. He could die here, let himself sink to the pavement, forget his troubles, wade into the waters of the other side.

Gianni thought of Franklin. *Will you be okay?* he'd asked, worried about Gianni's safety. If he had the energy, he'd laugh. Maybe Oswald would kill him after all. Maybe that would be fine.

Or he could say please.

Fuck it.

Gianni opened his eyes and stared at his tormentor, defeated. "Please," he whispered.

"That's what I thought."

Oswald scooped him up into impossibly strong arms, and his mouth returned to the wound—gentle this time, licking the torn flesh closed. Soft kisses dropped along the column of Gianni's throat. Loathsome. Gianni used his remaining strength to flinch from the vulgar touch, moist and sticky like syrup.

"See, that wasn't so hard. Stubborn thing. Here…"

He pushed Gianni's face into his neck, offering himself. Gianni desperately wanted to resist renewing their bond, but it was hopeless. Oswald had drained him, and he needed the stronger vampire's blood to live.

He opened his mouth and bit down hard.

4

THE LIBRARY

Gianni

ianni, still dazed, found himself in Oswald's arms being carried back to the Farthing and put to bed in his room. Clenching his eyes shut, Gianni tried to pull the covers over his face. Oswald's hand stopped him. Then a cold kiss pressed against his lips. "There, there, sleep tight, pet." Oswald stroked a wayward curl behind his ear. "That wasn't so bad, was it?"

Gianni was too weak to respond, though Oswald never listened to what he said anyway. He left after that, thank god, and Gianni passed out.

When he woke, he was alone, feeling like his sanctuary had been violated. The thought of Oswald in his rooms made his gut churn. Other vampires would have seen them. Together. Gianni in Oswald's arms. They would hate him even more now. Jealousy did that to people. If they only knew.

If he was going to slip out before the others woke, he needed to hurry. There was no time to pretty himself up for the slayer. Besides, his heart wasn't in it. Gianni didn't feel pretty; he felt used. He threw on dark jeans, track shoes, and a t-shirt. Would Buffy even recognize him?

Pausing to look in the mirror was a mistake. Purple bruising spread across his neck, the bitemark still pink and irritated. Perfect. Makeup would never hide it, and the damage was too high on his throat for a jacket to cover. Gianni chose a black silk scarf from his collection, less ridiculous with this outfit than the others. Before hurrying out, he wrapped it around his neck.

The slayer would have questions Gianni didn't want to answer.

Arriving at the library, he glanced around and didn't see Buffy but knew he was there. It felt like those first few days: the sensation of being watched, a tingle down his spine. Rather than seek him out, Gianni pretended he hadn't noticed and went inside. He'd already given too much away, arriving at this hour, too early for vampires to be out on the streets. No need to let the slayer know he could sense his presence.

He returned the books from last week, chose new ones, and then settled into an armchair to read. Or more realistically, to stare at the same page until Buffy made an appearance. The slayer waited until after dark, which was telling. So Buffy didn't want him to know he'd seen the vampire out before twilight. Gianni would do well to remember they weren't playing for the same team.

The slayer approached and cast a shadow in the way of Gianni's light. "Um, hello."

"Hello." Gianni indicated the seat across from him with a tip of his head, and the slayer sat down. "Took you long enough to find me."

"Sorry?"

"It's okay." Gianni's gaze swept the slayer from head to foot, not that anything had changed. Work pants, moss-colored shirt, patrol boots; all function over fashion. Gianni wondered what he'd look like in something tailored to his lean muscular form. He'd be dashing in a suit—or in nothing at all.

"So are you all right?" the slayer whispered.

Simple question, loaded answer, but Gianni only said, "Yes."

"Who was that guy last night?"

"My ex. Oswald. Sovereign over Philly and inexplicably here in Bristol Springs."

"Sovereign? Your ex is a sovereign?" Buffy's voice rose.

"Shush. We're in a library." Gianni waved a hand. "Did you choose a book?"

Buffy shook his head and gazed at the stacks of books surrounding them but made no motion to get up and peruse the collection. His eyes returned to Gianni.

"Would you like me to choose one for you?"

"No, thanks." The slayer sat back, watching him.

"This is a library, Buffy. People read at libraries." Gianni dug in his bag, picked out a book, and handed it over. "You can't make moon eyes at me all night."

"I don't make moon eyes, whatever that is," he complained but took the book. "*Pride and Prejudice*? I've always thought this book sounded stuffy."

"It isn't."

"I'll take your word for it."

"You will do no such thing. Read it or choose something for yourself, but you can't just sit there. It's weird."

Dutifully, the slayer opened the book.

Franklin

It is a truth universally acknowledged...

Franklin stared at the page. Were they really going to spend the whole night reading? Apparently so. When Franklin went into the family business, at no point did he picture himself seated at a library reading books opposite a vampire. A vampire with a library card.

This wasn't what the Scourge meant when they tasked him with finding out what was different about this vampire. He could see it now: *Yeah, uh, Chief Darrow, the vampire enjoys romance novels and long walks in the park...* No, that wouldn't do. Now, information on a sovereign, however—that might be worth something, if he could get the vampire talking.

The library closed at nine PM. Franklin watched Gianni load up his bag full of books and prepare to leave. He hadn't exactly made much headway in *Pride and Prejudice*—too busy thinking—but if the vampire wanted him to read it, he would.

"Can I keep this?"

Surprise flashed across Gianni's features. "Be sure to return it on time. I'll not have you ruining my reputation at the library, Buffy."

"Of course."

They exited and strolled together toward the business district. The air was crisp and cool: summer giving way to autumn, Franklin's favorite time of year. When Gianni hadn't said anything in a while, Franklin realized starting the conversation was up to him.

"You're quiet this evening."

Gianni side-eyed him and kept walking. "We were at a library, Buffy."

"Yes, but even now."

"I'm thinking."

"About what?"

"Nothing interesting."

An obtuse answer, even for Gianni. Franklin pushed. "Tell me what happened with that guy last night, your ex."

Gianni gave a dramatic sigh. Right as Franklin thought he wouldn't answer, the vampire said, "He's just an ex who thinks he owns me." Gianni's hand fiddled with the scarf around his neck. "Nothing happened."

Gianni's tone was too serious. This vampire was never serious, always flirting and joking. Franklin stopped walking. "I don't believe you. Nothing happened?"

Gianni turned to face him. "So what if it did? You gonna slay him for me? A sovereign? I doubt it." The vampire scowled, his pretty features scrunched into an ugly sneer. "Oswald would chop you into pieces and feed you to his cats."

"He could try. What did he do to you?"

Gianni scoffed and rocked back on his heels.

Before the vampire could stop him, Franklin grabbed the loose end of Gianni's scarf and yanked. Gianni clenched his jaw and tried to cover his throat with his hand, spinning away quickly, but he wasn't fast enough. Franklin saw the damage, pink and red like raw meat.

"The fuck, Gianni? What the hell happened?"

"You should see the other guy," Gianni muttered, but Franklin would have none of it. He took the vampire by the shoulders and brought them face to face.

"What did he do to you?"

"I would think that much is obvious." Gianni pressed his lips into a thin line and narrowed his gaze.

"Did you let him do this?"

"Don't be stupid. Does this seem consensual?" Color rose in Gianni's cheeks; his eyes watered. He dropped his hand, letting Franklin look his fill.

It was bad. Franklin hadn't seen anything like it. Typically, when he saw a vampire bite, it was on a donor, and the feeding vampire would have closed the wound to encourage healing. Vampire bites normally healed quickly; it had to do with specialized enzymes in their saliva. This bite was brutal—ragged—and had barely begun to close. Red around the edges, there were signs of infection. That should be impossible. Vampires didn't get infections.

Gianni's gaze was distant. He looked ashamed. This wasn't the sassy vampire Franklin was coming to know.

In spite of all his training and everything he knew to be true about vampires, Franklin couldn't stand seeing Gianni so pitiful. He took a risk and opened his arms. Gianni hesitated, but only for a moment. Then Franklin found his arms full of sniffling vampire. He didn't know what to do next. He patted Gianni's back awkwardly. "Hey now, it's okay."

"It's really not."

"Tell me what happened."

Gianni took a deep breath against him. Franklin felt hands on his sides. This was dangerous. Gianni could kill him in an instant, but instead of pulling away, he forced himself to relax into the embrace.

"He made promises and broke them. I came off like a fool for believing him. He wanted to isolate me and make me friendless. He was good at it. There are things I shouldn't tell you—not that you believe anything I say anyway. Last night was just more of the same."

"You can tell me," Franklin offered. "If you want."

Gianni glanced up. For the first time, Franklin let the eye contact linger for more than a heartbeat. Gianni's eyes were hazel and glittered with moisture, like the forest after a storm. Beautiful. All the rules flew out the window. If the vampire wanted to hypnotize him, Franklin had just made it easy.

"What's your name?"

Franklin froze. He didn't feel compelled, so the vampire wasn't using his influence, simply asking. Regardless, Franklin shook his head.

"I can't. I—"

"Then I can't tell you, can I?" Gianni said sadly, dropping his arms and stepping back. Franklin let him go, the warmth where they'd been pressed together cooling with the night air.

Gianni wiped his eyes, and Franklin saw his composure returning in stages.

"See you around, Buffy." He walked away.

It was a dismissal, but Franklin longed to follow. He wanted to help, but he also, finally, had something useful to report to the Scourge.

Franklin left in the opposite direction, knowing he would come back during business hours and get his own damn library card.

5

REJECTION

Gianni

Oswald lingered around the Farthing. His presence forced Gianni to lay low—not something he had much experience with, but a necessary evil to escape the man's attention. He didn't want to run into the sovereign. More than that, he didn't want the temptation to drink from him again. If Oswald thought the renewal of their blood bond would entice Gianni to follow him home, tail between his legs, he was wrong. Now Gianni suffered the pain of withdrawal as Oswald's powerful blood worked its way from his system—again—but being free of him was worth it.

The nasty wound on his neck healed slowly. If he had been an undead vampire like the others, it would be gone already, but his living body needed nights to repair this kind of damage. Oswald had made sure it would linger, biting deep, tearing muscle and flesh. He'd wanted to remind Gianni that his body wasn't his own. Gianni avoided mirrors. Seeing the marks made his stomach churn.

Surely the sovereign had responsibilities back in Philly.

Gianni would wait him out, stay holed up in his room with his library books until the asshole left. Hopefully by then he would feel better, and his neck would be healed.

The alone time made him restless, and he spent a lot of it thinking of the slayer. Buffy had given him a hug, offered comfort. How much was real and how much only deception? The man was hard to read, but something in his eyes drew Gianni to him, despite the danger. Maybe because of it. Buffy's arms had been stiff around him, his posture rigid, perhaps ready to spring at any moment. Putting himself in the slayer's arms had been a risk, but he'd needed the comfort more than he feared an attack.

A slayer should be kept at arm's length, so wanting to run his fingers through his pretty brown hair wasn't helpful. Conflict had shone in the slayer's enticing gaze, and Gianni wasn't sure if he stood on the winning side of the battle. The Scourge had a tight hold over their slayers. Buffy had his own motives, but Gianni couldn't fathom them. If the Scourge ordered his death, what would the slayer do? Gianni wasn't confident of the answer.

A knock sounded at his door.

Oswald.

Gianni had no friends in Bristol Springs to come calling. The sovereign had left him alone all week, but not out of kindness. Oswald had counted on Gianni seeking him out for blood.

Damn. This wouldn't be pretty.

Thankfully, he was dressed down in lounging sweats and a t-shirt—the sort of clothes Oswald had never let him wear. He added a scarf over the bite wound for good measure. He wouldn't allow the sadist to get pleasure from ogling the damage.

How could he get rid of him? Quickly, Gianni cluttered up his neat room, scattering books and throwing clothes around.

Though hunkering down and hiding was tempting, not

answering the door wasn't an option. Oswald was an older vampire, powerful; he could smell Gianni from outside. If the door wasn't opened, he'd kick it in.

Gianni was reaching for the door when the knock came again, harder this time, as if even a knock could be angry. He opened it and stood in the frame, casually blocking Oswald's entry.

"Did I wake you?" Oswald looked down on Gianni through half-opened lids, like he was already bored.

Let the Oswald show begin.

"Lazy to be sleeping at this hour." Oswald tutted—a clicking sound in the back of his throat Gianni had learned to despise, the sort you'd make to lead a horse.

Oswald had come alone, which didn't bode well for the outcome.

No witnesses.

He wore a suit in shades of orange, mostly rust and copper, and carried a walking stick for reasons Gianni would rather not fathom.

"I was reading. What do you want?"

"Aren't you going to invite me in?"

"The room isn't up to your standards. You won't appreciate the mess." Gianni hoped that would be enough of a deterrent. It wasn't.

Oswald shouldered past him, knocking him off balance as he strode into the apartment. "When did you become a slob?"

Gianni left the door hanging open and followed. He didn't bother to answer the question because Oswald only asked it to hear the sound of his own voice. He never cared about Gianni's reply.

Oswald took a seat on the bed, crossed his legs, set the cane on them, and stared a hard line at Gianni. "I came to help you pack."

"I'm not leaving." Gianni stood near the door, hands on hips, wary.

"Nonsense. You've wasted enough of my time. I need to get back to Philly." He smoothed his hands down his thighs and glanced around. "Where's your suitcase?"

"I'm staying here." To his own ears, Gianni sounded confident. If only he could feel it too.

Oswald stood. "On second thought, leave it all here." He peered at the clutter distastefully. "I'll buy you new things when we get home."

Gianni shook his head. "I'm not going with you."

Voice rising, Oswald stalked toward him. "Stop being ridiculous. You'll do as I say."

Gianni took a step back, closer to the open door.

"I've been lenient with you, and my patience is reaching its limit." Oswald only stopped when they were toe to toe.

"This isn't the 1800s. You don't own me." Gianni had his back to the wall. "I don't want to go with you, and you can't force me."

Quick as a viper, Oswald pinned Gianni to the wall by his throat. "Can't I?" He began to lift the smaller man off his feet.

Gianni raised both hands to Oswald's but couldn't budge them. Or breathe. The hallway stood empty, and he couldn't call out anyway. Struggling only made it worse. Realizing he wouldn't be able to think his way out of this, panic set in. Gianni pleaded for mercy with his eyes.

"Admit it, little one, you miss me," Oswald snarled, flinging spit into Gianni's face. "No one can give you the kind of pounding you need as well as I can. You must be starved for it by now." Oswald kissed him hard.

Despite the violence, fear made Gianni open his mouth for Oswald's tongue. He'd fake it, moan and whimper the way Oswald liked it, but sound was impossible without air. Lightheaded, he began to pass out.

Before blackness took hold, Oswald dropped him to his feet and released his neck.

Gianni drew in deep, gasping breaths and fought to stay upright. The urge to double over was strong, but he'd rather fall on his face than let Oswald catch him. He leaned against the wall for support.

"Come home, and I'll forgive you. There won't be any trouble." Oswald ran a finger down his cheek.

Gianni wanted to vomit. He couldn't say *no*, not with his throat burning, but he shook his head slowly, staring at the floor. If Oswald wanted to take him, he'd have to throw Gianni over his shoulder, kicking and screaming the length of the Farthing. Others would see.

Oswald could pretend the laws didn't apply to him, but they did.

Gianni caught his breath as he waited for whatever came next. Words rarely failed him, but he could think of nothing to say to defuse the situation or make Oswald leave any faster. The stubborn sovereign wouldn't go until he decided this wasn't worth his time.

Just be boring.

Oswald let out an exasperated sigh. "You never did know what was best for you. I worry for you here, on your own." Oswald petted Gianni's head and cupped his cheek. "What will happen to you without my guidance?"

A number of snippy replies rushed to the tip on Gianni's tongue. *Be boring.* He stared dully at Oswald's ridiculous tie. Orange paisley. Hideous.

"No one likes you here. They think you're a gold-digger and revile you for doing what they could not. You won me over, little bird, and now you're mine." Oswald kissed him again, sweet and feather-soft this time.

Gianni made no protest, but he did not return the kiss. Cool lips parted his warmth. Oswald's tongue traced his fangs, and a bright coppery drop of blood set Gianni's taste buds aflame. He sucked the wounded tongue into his mouth to chase the flavor, but the cut had already healed.

"Leave with me and revel in their jealousy as you cling to my arm." He whispered the words against the flushed skin of Gianni's cheek. "I promise to look smitten."

This softening was unexpected. It wouldn't work, but perhaps Gianni could use it to his advantage. He reached for Oswald's chest, palming the muscles beneath his hands.

"Thank you, Ozzy, but I can't." Gianni slid his hands to Oswald's shoulders. "I need to be alone for a while to figure myself out. Even if everyone hates me. I can't expect you to take care of me forever." He gazed up through his lashes. "It's time I learned to do it myself."

Oswald pressed his lips into a thin line.

This could go either way. Gianni's heartbeat thundered in his ears.

Oswald stepped out of his reach. "When you tire of this experiment, youngling, you know where to find me. I shall not turn you away, but neither can I promise to be so welcoming next time."

"Thank you." Relief threatened to set in, but Gianni forced it back. "Have a safe trip home."

"Try not to do anything stupid while I'm too far away to save you."

Gianni nodded.

Oswald left.

With the door closed and locked, Gianni allowed himself a few deep breaths. A glimmer of relief waited to envelope him with its sweetness, but he wouldn't relax until the sovereign and his entourage had left the Farthing completely. Gianni picked up his things and set the room back in order. He needed control over something, if only a tidy apartment.

Oswald left Bristol Springs as promised. Gianni went to bed that morning on a high of relief, feeling safer and more secure than he had all week.

That evening he woke up lonely and restless. Again, his thought turned to the slayer. Gianni longed to be near him. Their verbal sparring kept him on his toes, and he missed the stomach flutters Buffy's presence stirred in him.

Gianni left the Farthing to seek him out. Better to tease Buffy in person than to pine after him alone in his room. What started as merely an interesting game had somehow become… significant. A wiser man would quit while he was ahead, but that wasn't in Gianni's nature.

Wandering the familiar streets of Bristol Springs, sensing the slayer's presence didn't take long. Rounding the corner from 6th onto Main Street, by the jeweler he wished was open at night, Gianni glanced up and grinned.

"Stop lurking. I know you're there," he called.

Buffy jumped down from the shadows.

Franklin

From his perch atop a fire escape, he spotted Gianni moments before the vampire called to him, luring him down to the street. Gianni appeared more himself tonight, his posture perfect, his clothes immaculate and showy. Back in blacks, he wore a fitted charcoal sweater hanging low over dark leggings. Something in the fabric glittered under the street light. Jewelry decorated his wrists and fingers, and his hair lay carefully arranged off his forehead, styled, but not over the top. His bright face remained makeup-free, smiling as Franklin drew near.

This was the second time Franklin had gone a full week before spotting the vampire, but just when Franklin was sure Gianni had left town and he'd be reassigned, the vampire turned up as if nothing was amiss. During his absence, Franklin had meted out what little information he'd gleaned from Gianni—that the Sovereign of Philadelphia was in town, that Gianni didn't heal like other vampires. It bought him some time with Chief Darrow, but he'd need more soon, or they might stage the live capture early. He'd only been given a month, and time was running out. If he didn't act soon, Franklin could miss his chance to lead the team.

Or his chance to warn Gianni.

He pushed the thought aside as ludicrous.

"Good evening." Gianni stepped in, too close for comfort, as usual.

Franklin nodded and had to root his feet to the ground not to step back. Last time he'd seen Gianni, he'd held the vampire in his arms, but a week had gone by with no word, and now being this close felt risky again. The sovereign could have brain-washed him in that time.

"Hello, Gianni. How are you?"

"Much better now, thank you. You?" Gianni was peering up at him through long lashes.

Franklin avoided meeting his gaze, which left him staring at his lips instead. That wasn't any better.

"Fine, thank you."

"Formal tonight." Gianni indicated they should walk together. "Shall we?"

Gianni could lead him into a trap. The vampire made him reckless. He let the thought pass.

"Sure." They set off at a leisurely pace into town.

It was quiet, the night sounds dampened by a mist that hung in the air and threatened rain. Franklin liked this weather. It usually meant a slow night.

"Oswald's gone back to Philly," Gianni said.

"Good riddance."

"You can say that again."

Franklin glanced over at his throat, checking on the bitemark. He tried to be discreet, but Gianni noticed and tilted his neck for inspection. "All better."

"Mostly better," Franklin amended. New pink skin covered the wound, looking tender like a human's. *Strange.*

"Mostly better," Gianni conceded.

"Why were you with him, if he was such a jerk?"

"He wasn't always a jerk, Buffy. That's how they get ya. It's all roses and blowjobs at first, and wham." Gianni clapped once. "The controlling bastard makes an appearance. By then, you're hooked. Then again, maybe you don't know. Maybe all of your relationships have been nice."

"Relationships?" He scoffed. "No time for them."

"You don't date?"

"I've had flings, one-night stands, but never relationships. Women tend to want more than I can give them."

"Women."

"Right."

"No men?"

"I'm not exactly gay."

"What does that mean?"

"Well, I don't date much, but when I do, I see women."

"But you aren't exactly straight, either?"

Franklin didn't have an answer. He'd been attracted to other men before Gianni, but dating women was easier. He didn't talk about this. Blood rushed to his cheeks. He'd paused too long, and the silence got weird. "Not exactly."

"I can work with that."

Oh my god. Something about that statement made Gianni's whimsical flirting feel more serious. When he wasn't actively denying it, Franklin realized they'd been heading in that direction from the beginning.

"Let's go out," Gianni said.

"What do you mean, go out? We are out."

"Well, I am. You're apparently not. But I meant let's go out on a date. On purpose. Instead of aimlessly wandering around night after night." Gianni gestured to their surroundings, the quiet, dimly lit streets of Bristol Springs.

Franklin hesitated. *A date? Dressing up, maybe a nice dinner— no. Vampires couldn't go out to dinner. Dancing then? Or a movie? Could he do that?* "Um, okay."

"So tomorrow night? Dancing?"

Franklin gave a small nod. What was he getting himself into?

"I can't tell if that meant, yes, I'll be there, or no thanks, I'd rather alphabetize the contents of my cabinets."

"Yes, I'll be there."

"Good." Gianni smiled. "Oh, and Buffy?"

"Yeah?"

"Wear something nice."

Holy shit.

6

DANCING

Gianni

The Mint Lounge felt overly warm and the music too quiet for Gianni's taste. This was a human club. The vampire establishments were nicer, but Gianni couldn't bring a slayer there. He would be out of place *here*; imagining him at The Den was absurd.

Gianni had gotten there early, already dancing with a musclebound blond dreamboat when Buffy shuffled in. Good, maybe he could make the slayer jealous. He leaned tighter to the stranger's chest, waiting to be noticed.

Buffy spotted them and gave a nod in his direction, along with a half-smile. Gianni grinned back, excusing himself from the dance. When the slayer looked *like that*, jealousy was over-rated. Edible. He'd dressed up, as requested. The effect was immediate. Gianni was drawn to him and feeling handsy.

Dress slacks accentuated his lean legs and showed off well-shaped thighs, paired with a casual but striking fitted green top bringing out the color of his eyes. The muscles of his chest and biceps strained the thin fabric. Who knew Buffy was hiding *that* under his frumpy delivery-driver clothes? The picture he presented was devastating. Some less-than-professional-quality product slicked back his chestnut hair, of which Gianni immediately disapproved, but A for effort. He wanted to ravish him; those fine clothes would look even better scattered across his floor.

"Hello, handsome." Gianni approached, leaning in to offer his cheek. Buffy got the idea, and dry lips kissed Gianni so lightly he could almost have imagined it. He slid his hands over the slayer's ribcage, cataloguing each intercostal muscle under his fingertips. "You sure clean up nice."

"Thank you." Buffy let himself be petted. He didn't pet back.

Gianni was showing a lot of skin and knew the slayer would be unsure how to touch him. He'd thought it would be amusing but found himself wishing he'd made things simpler. A nice blouse instead of the racerback top he'd chosen to show off his shoulders. Next time.

"Buy me a drink?" Gianni asked, indicating the bar.

"Um, sure." Buffy led them through the crowd of dancing couples. This wasn't exclusively a gay club, but other same-sex pairings moved among the patrons. Gianni thought the mix would make Buffy more comfortable.

The bartender wore flaming orange lipstick to match her neon orange hair.

Buffy turned to Gianni. "What do you want a drink for?"

"What do you mean what for? The usual reasons. Whiskey, please and thank you."

The slayer asked Orange Lipstick for the drink but only ordered one. Gianni called after her, "Two, please." She nodded and grabbed a second glass.

"Oh, I'm not drinking."

"Why not?"

Buffy opened his mouth to answer, but Gianni held up his hand. "And do not tell me you're working."

Buffy closed his mouth and looked down.

"Oh my god, are you seriously working right now? You dick."

The slayer shook his head. "No, no. I'm really not. They don't know I'm here. It's just… Well, I feel like I'm always working. It's my default state of being. I need to be sober and on guard at all times."

"That's pathetic."

Buffy shrugged.

Orange Lipstick returned with their drinks.

Gianni picked his up and motioned for the slayer to do the same. Buffy's eyebrows lifted, but he raised the glass and clinked it with Gianni's.

"Cheers," Gianni said.

"Wait, you can't actually drink that." Buffy lowered his voice to a whisper. "Vampires can't have anything but blood."

"Watch me." Gianni tipped back his glass and took a swallow, warming his throat with a pleasant burn. "Now you. Bottoms up, Buffy."

The slayer took a drink. "There. Now, are you going to explain?"

"Nope."

"But—"

Gianni shook his head. "We're not talking about that. Finish your drink and ask me to dance." Gianni took another sip. It wasn't as smooth as he liked, but loosening Buffy up would be worth it.

Buffy polished off the whiskey and hesitated.

Gianni took pity on him, holding out his hand. "Go on. It's not as if I'll say no."

The slayer, a half-smile on his face, took it. "I'm not any good at this, but would you like to dance?"

"I'd be delighted." Gianni let Buffy lead him onto the floor and had to stifle a laugh when Buffy lifted their clasped hands to shoulder height and placed his other gingerly on Gianni's waist. Gianni had never been to a junior prom, so now was as good a time as any. He went with it, resting his hand on the Slayer's shoulder as surely the man expected.

"This is the only type of dancing you know, isn't it?"

"Um, yeah. Sorry."

"You're doing fine. Just relax and enjoy it."

They swayed to music meant for grinding, but Gianni didn't care. Being in their own little world was good. He stepped in close enough to feel the heat of the slayer's body but didn't press against it. Yet.

"You know, it's crowded here. We're safe...you can't slay me...I can't bite you." Gianni let his fingertips trail over the soft skin on the back of the slayer's hand. "We could dance a little closer."

When Buffy didn't protest, Gianni wrapped his arm around his neck and brought their chests together. Gianni could smell his aftershave, and underneath it, his natural scent. Ripe pears and honey. Buffy let it happen, but he didn't relax, his shoulders tense under Gianni's fingers. To distract him, Gianni asked, "Are you still reading the book?"

"I finished it."

That was surprising. "Really? How did you like it?"

"Not what I'd normally read, though you were right. Not stuffy."

Gianni leaned in closer. In this position, his mouth was next to the slayer's neck. A tempting blue vein pulsed underneath the smooth skin. Gianni wanted to lick it. He wanted to do more than lick it.

"Why'd you choose it?" the slayer asked.

"Choose what?" Gianni responded, lost in his desire.

"The book. *Pride and Prejudice.*"

Oh, right. That. "I wanted us to have something to talk about while you're deciding whether or not to kill me, and I'm tolerating it because, unlike you, I don't actually kill."

"You're a vampire. Of course you kill."

"No, actually, I don't."

"I don't believe you."

Gianni rolled his eyes. "Probably because you've killed so much you think it's normal."

"I don't kill *people*. I kill *vampires*. And I don't for one second believe you'd go hungry to preserve human life."

"Then you'd underestimate me, but you're right—I don't go hungry. I also don't have to kill to eat. None of us do. We don't need that much blood. You have to stop believing everything they tell you."

"You've never killed anyone? Not even accidentally?"

"How do you accidentally kill someone? Is that a thing?"

"I didn't mean it like that." The slayer backpedaled and put some distance between them.

"How many vampires have you killed?" Gianni asked.

The slayer didn't answer. They stopped dancing.

"You're quick to accuse me of murder, but quiet when I call you out. You're the monster here, not me. They feed you lies, and you kill based on those lies. Not proof." At this point, keeping his voice down was a struggle.

"Bloodless corpses aren't proof? Dead and drained people whose faces are frozen in terror? That's not proof? I've seen proof."

"We're not all like that." Gianni pulled the slayer back in tight. He didn't want to look into his eyes anymore, not when they were angry.

The dance music throbbed. A heavy silence sat between the two men, their heartbeats elevated, pounding against each other. Gianni took a deep breath and willed himself calm. Buffy copied the gesture—whether conscious or not, Gianni didn't know.

Gianni broke the stalemate. "Why me?"

"I don't know."

"If they give you orders to kill me, will you do it?"

"If I had orders to kill you, you'd be dead."

"Or you'd be."

"I thought you didn't kill people."

"I'm thinking of making an exception." Gianni nipped his earlobe, and the slayer startled, but recovered when Gianni didn't draw blood. They continued to dance. The music changed, but their delicate sway did not. So close, and yet still so much distance.

Gianni whispered in the slayer's ear, "I'm going to convince you not to kill me before they order you to do it. I don't want to fight you."

"You never answered my question."

It was an obvious change of subject, but Gianni let it slide. Things had gotten too heated between them. "What question?"

"The book. Why'd you pick *Pride and Prejudice?*"

"You look like how I've always pictured Mr. Darcy. Tall, brown hair, green eyes. Handsome. Arrogant. Clueless. You remind me of him. That's why I chose it for you. That, and every library is guaranteed to have a copy."

"Clueless?" Buffy complained without any real venom.

"And handsome," Gianni soothed.

"Can we get out of here?"

"Now you're talking."

"No, that's not what—"

"Joking. Relax. Let's go."

They left the club for the cool night air, Gianni's hand tucked snug in the slayer's elbow.

If they leaned into each other, if their steps matched in rhythm—well. What a lovely coincidence.

If another slayer happened to be watching them, though, that would be a nasty break.

7

NEW MISSION

Franklin

The ghost of Gianni's touch lingered long after the vampire said goodnight. Franklin felt him against his chest, warm waist under his palm. He shook his head to clear it. The situation was getting out of hand. Franklin never understood why some humans found vampires alluring, until now. He *liked* this saucy vampire. From Gianni's curious nature to his witty needling, to the feline motion of his hips under Franklin's hands—all of it.

At the Foundry, Franklin joined Hutch in Darrow's office to give his report. There was nothing to say, but the chief would expect an update. The more he thought about it, the more he wanted to tell Gianni to get out while he still could. Where would that leave Franklin? He hadn't realized how lonely he'd been until he wasn't. He couldn't imagine life without Gianni.

"Lieutenants," Darrow greeted from his seat behind the desk. "What do I need to know?"

Hutch eyed Franklin suspiciously, lips tight, brow raised. Holding back wasn't like the man. Usually, he jumped at the chance to speak first, and tonight Franklin needed him to. He wanted more time to decide what to tell the chief. When neither man spoke up, Darrow chose for them.

"Denhart, report."

Damn it.

Franklin stuck as close to the truth as he could. "I spotted Gianni at a human dance club called the Mint Lounge. I assumed he was hunting, but he left alone. I tailed him—"

"He left alone?" said Hutch.

Franklin ignored the interruption and plowed forward. "I've yet to see him with a donor or a kill. He must prefer to dine alone, or maybe at the Farthing, I don't know."

"You don't know?" Hutch sniped.

"What's that supposed to mean?"

"Gentlemen," said Darrow. "Enough. What are you getting at, Wilson?"

"I saw them, sir. Leaving the club. *Together.*"

Franklin froze in place. He'd left the club with Gianni practically hanging off his fucking arm. His mind raced to come up with an explanation.

Hutch continued, "They were acting like they knew each other. The vampire was touching him."

"What?" said Darrow. "Denhart, what is he talking about?"

It was now or never. "I'm sorry, sir. I didn't think you'd approve my plan, so I kept it to myself. I was going to tell you when I had more information. I'm almost there."

"Almost where?" said Hutch. "In his pants?"

"I'm not going to warn you again," ordered Darrow, scowling.

Hutch let out a harsh breath through his nose but stayed silent.

Darrow turned his full attention to Franklin. "Explain yourself, Lieutenant."

Franklin squared his shoulders and forced confidence he did

not feel into his voice. "The vampire, Gianni, has been speaking to me ever since he caught me watching him two weeks ago. I don't know why he didn't attack, but I couldn't because we need him alive. In the stalemate, we began having conversations. I've encouraged a friendship. He...*flirts* with me."

Hutch snickered. Franklin pressed on. "I'm using it to learn things about him. He told me more about the sovereign. He's unintentionally revealed his own weakness as far as healing and recovery. Oswald bit him, and the wound didn't heal like we'd expect. I think he'll tell me more. He's beginning to trust me. Gianni may be more human than vampire. I aim to find out." Franklin had to grit his teeth and make himself say the next bit. "The more I know, the easier the live capture will be."

Darrow leaned back in his chair. "This is dangerous ground you're on, Denhart. Unprecedented. What would your father say?"

"I know, sir. It seemed the best strategy at the time. I believe I made the right choice." Franklin prepared for the worst. He could be removed from the mission, even demoted for his breach of protocol.

Darrow considered him. Hutch stared at them both, obviously itching to speak, but kept his mouth shut. The chief finally nodded. "Continue on this course, Lieutenant, but be careful. Human traits or not, he's a vampire. Don't get complacent around him."

"Yes, sir."

Hutch's jaw dropped open.

Franklin wouldn't gloat, but he wanted to.

"Keep him close," Darrow ordered. "Do whatever you have to do. We'll get more information out of him this way, willingly, before handing him over for interrogation. This is a unique opportunity. Take as much time as you need. Dismissed."

Relief filled his chest along with a rush of elation. Franklin had as much time to spend with Gianni as he liked. Except, if he was being realistic, that wasn't much time at all. How long could he drag the mission out before Darrow would insist on seizing Gianni?

A sinking feeling in the pit of his stomach, Franklin left Hutch and Darrow to whatever they had to discuss.

Imagining Gianni imprisoned and interrogated made him cringe. If Franklin went through with it, he might finally make his father proud, but at what cost?

Gianni

Finding a blood donor was a simple matter of filling out paper-work and being matched with a willing candidate. Gianni thought the process revolting, too much like a dating app. Of course, the alternate method required him to network with other vampires, explore the city himself, or build his own rela-tionships in the human community, all pursuits requiring socializing. Social ladders hadn't done him any favors. He'd given them up cold turkey. Except for the slayer, that was, but picturing Buffy donating blood to a vampire was like expecting something authentic from a reality TV show. Impossible, however satisfying to think about.

The slayer would be sweet and decadent, like he smelled. He'd be tense at first, though Gianni would ease him into it until he relaxed. Until he begged for it.

With a sigh, Gianni pushed the fantasy aside and made his way to the woman he'd been paired with, Tabea Perez. Careful to avoid his usual haunts, Gianni took side roads to her place. He couldn't risk running into Buffy. This wasn't something he wanted the slayer to see.

Tabea's profile said she was a grad student earning cash from her blood donations to pay for school. Gianni chose her specifically because she wasn't interested in sex. She had a boyfriend, and random hookups with vampires weren't her thing. Thank god. Most every other donor would expect some sort of…favor.

No money would change hands. The council arranged it all, a service Gianni took advantage of to deposit payment directly into her account, no awkward transactions necessary. Easy peasy.

How did one greet someone he was about to feed from but not have sex with? This was new terrain for Gianni. In Philly, he'd had Oswald pulling these strings, and the sex made everything obvious. One interaction bled into the next, no need to think. Simply do.

This was different. Would there be small talk first? Should he ask how her day was? Would she want to know about his? Gianni rolled his neck until it made a satisfying pop and knocked on her door. Get it over with. He needed blood. She needed money. How difficult could it be?

The young woman opened the door with a smile on her face and a spoon in her hand. "Hey, you must be Gianni. Come on in, I'm just getting dinner into the instant pot." She left the door wide open and headed back into the house, indicating a tidy living room, albeit small. "Make yourself at home. I'll be right over."

As she left, Gianni got a good look at her. Gray leggings and t-shirt advertising some 5k run. Fit. Casual. Gianni could do casual. Her house smelled delicious, like cooked onions and maybe beef stew, something hearty and welcoming.

Gianni sat on the couch and scanned the room. Textbooks were scattered about, but the place itself was clean, sparsely decorated, and modern. No TV. Lots of plants. It had 'millennial' written all over it.

Tabea strode back into the room and plopped down next to him, hand extended. "Sorry about that. I'm Tabea."

Gianni shook her offered hand and returned the smile. "Gianni. Pleased to meet you. Thank you for having me."

"No problem. You hungry?" She moved her lovely black hair over her shoulder, gathering it in a quick twist and tucking it into itself and out of the way. Smooth olive skin beckoned. Suddenly, Gianni *was* quite hungry.

"We don't have to talk about the weather first?"

Tabea laughed, her ease settling Gianni's nerves. "Fucking humid, right? What happened to fall?"

Gianni laughed with her. He already liked Tabea. What was she studying? "Indeed."

"It's really okay. You're not my first match. I know what to expect. You can just go ahead if you want. I know you probably have other things to do."

"I really don't. But I'm sure you do, so thank you. I'll be quick." Gianni leaned in. Tabea tilted her head to give him room, and her hand closed over his shoulder. He took that as permission to touch her as well, his hand gently cradling the back of her head as he let his fangs drop.

He bit. Divine. She was perfect. Hot and spicy. Thick healthy blood filled his mouth and coated his throat. Tabea hadn't flinched. She relaxed her neck and let Gianni support the weight of her head as he drank. Definitely not new to this.

It'd been too long. He shouldn't have gone weeks without finding a donor. Now he wanted more than he should take. Reluctantly, he slipped his teeth from her flesh and lapped at the wound until the skin closed, leaving two pink marks that would fade overnight. He kissed her cheek before releasing her head and leaning out of her space. "Thank you."

Tabea gave his shoulder a squeeze before falling back into the cushions with a sigh. "You betcha."

The rush of her blood filling his veins made him shiver. He followed her lead and settled deeper into the couch, his body feeling temporarily boneless.

"What are you studying?"

"Molecular biophysics."

"Shit. That sounds hard."

"Not so hard. Expensive, though."

Gianni nodded, but he didn't believe her. It must be hard. He'd been wasting his life sleeping his way to the top—which hadn't even worked—while this woman put herself through college and now grad school in a field he couldn't even define. This reality check was probably overdue, but the pill wasn't easy to swallow.

"Your dinner smells delicious." Food. He could probably manage to discuss food.

"Oh thanks, I've been trying to eat better. Doctor's orders. One too many microwave pizzas has raised my blood pressure. I'd offer you some, but—I mean, you know."

"Are you serious, because I'm starving, and believe it or not, I can definitely eat your food." His mouth was watering at the prospect. "I can also arrange to pay you more. Do you think I could come back next week?"

"I thought food made vampires sick? And yeah, next week is cool."

"It won't make me sick. It smells like heaven."

"Well, there's plenty. Hopefully it tastes as good as it smells." She stood and loosened her hair, letting it fall around her shoulders in waves. "Come on, then."

Gianni followed her into the kitchen where she was already setting out an extra plate for him.

"Is your boyfriend home? Will this be awkward?"

"No, and no. He works nights. If he was here, he'd talk your head off. He didn't know about vampires until we got serious. I mean, most humans don't, so I wouldn't have expected him to. He took it really well, and now he's fucking fascinated. He'd ask you all kinds of nosy questions. Don't worry about it."

"How did *you* know?"

"My great-uncle is a vampire. He was in his twenties when he was changed, so I call him cousin. My whole family knows. I was a kid when they told me. It's just ordinary for us."

Gianni nodded. Tabea's nonchalance was fascinating. He'd been so wrapped up in vampire culture; befriending a human never occurred to him. Other than Buffy.

"So what do you do?" she asked, stirring whatever smelled so good in the instant pot, the aroma even stronger now with the lid open. Gianni had hit the jackpot with this match. He wouldn't knock the system anymore.

"I don't know. Nothing worthwhile. What should I do?"

Tabea's laugh was becoming familiar. "How should I know? Whatever vampires do, I guess."

"Write poetry and skulk in shadows?" Gianni suggested.

"Maybe you need a life coach."

"Maybe I do."

8

SPIKE

Franklin

Some nights, Gianni was easy to find, and others, Franklin wandered around for hours with no luck. The last few nights the vampire was nowhere to be found, and tonight was proving the same. With official approval for their bizarre relationship, he was dying to put it to good use. Maybe he'd ask Gianni for his number. Could he do that? It would make things simple. His father would never believe it.

How are you keeping tabs on that vampire, son?

Oh, it's no big deal. I text him.

Right.

He couldn't share this mission with his father. Not until it was finished. And if he decided to warn Gianni and the vampire fled, not ever.

Franklin brooded over the consequences of coming clean. Like most things concerning the vampire, it was tempting. At first, Gianni would be furious, but once Franklin explained, he'd come around.

Probably. Maybe. *Or not.*

Gianni was stubborn; after the initial blow-up, he might not stick around to listen to reason. Or they might fight. It wasn't Franklin's fault he was a vampire hunter, and Gianni *was* a vampire. Since this whole mess started with a mission, Gianni must have suspected something. Hopefully, the fighting would stick to words and not bleed out into action.

Maybe Franklin should tell him in a letter.

That way, there would be no face-to-face explosion. Gianni would have time to calm down before they met again. If they met again.

Eventually, the vampire would understand, and he would flee for his life. He'd never get taken by the Scourge. He would be safe. The Scourge never had to find out Franklin had tipped him off to their plans. Franklin would go back to his regular patrol schedule. Life would get back to normal.

Life would be boring.

Or Franklin could go through with the mission. Let the Scourge capture Gianni and keep the vampire in their labs. Franklin would get a promotion, and his father would be proud. He'd always know where the vampire was, and he could visit whenever he wanted.

Gianni would hate him.

He'd hate himself.

And worse, what would they do to him? Whatever happened, it would be Franklin's fault.

There was no good answer. Franklin would be alone either way, but he would get used to it. He was good at being alone before Gianni, and he'd be good at it after. Not that they were together, because that would be ridiculous.

Franklin ruminated until he spotted the vampire down a side street. Gianni was inexplicably on his knees, focused on something behind a dumpster and making clucking noises. *What the hell?*

Gianni's head turned as Franklin approached, his finger over his lips warning him to stay quiet. How the vampire knew he was there, Franklin wasn't sure. It was well past midnight and dark out. No streetlights lit the alley. Right when he thought the vampire couldn't get weirder, Gianni began cooing toward a stinking pile of trash.

"What's going on?"

Gianni shushed him and continued speaking to whatever was behind the dumpster. "It's okay. Come on. That's only my friend Buffy. He's supposed to be scary, but he's not, I promise." The vampire sighed, and his shoulders drooped. "Damn it." He stood, brushed off his knees, and glared at Franklin. "I almost had her, but you scared her away. Now I'll have to start over."

"Had who? What are you doing?"

Gianni stepped aside. "See for yourself."

Franklin came forward and peered behind the dumpster. A small shaggy dog was squeezed as far back as it could get, out of reach and cowering. "A dog."

"Yes. A dog. And I almost had her before you showed up. Now she's hiding again."

Franklin crouched to get a better view. "Well, hello there." He held out his hand. The dog watched him but remained in place, shivering. Probably some sort of spaniel mix, thin and dirty, no collar. Not aggressive, but too afraid to be friendly. "It's probably hungry."

"She."

"How do you know?"

Gianni shrugged. "I don't. Calling her an 'it' feels callous."

"She, then," Franklin agreed and stood. "Do you have any food for her?"

Gianni rolled his eyes. "Would you believe I managed to leave *without* my spare bag of dog food tonight?"

"So, that's a no."

"I thought about getting some, but I didn't want to leave her alone."

"I'll do it. We'll need a car, too."

"A car?"

"To take her to a shelter."

"Oh."

"What was your plan?"

"No plan, exactly. I just couldn't leave her." Gianni gazed back at the mess of quivering fur behind the dumpster.

"Stay here. I'll be back in thirty." Franklin turned to go.

"Buffy?"

Franklin paused, glancing over his shoulder.

"Thank you."

Franklin nodded and cast a lingering glance at the vampire. Gianni stood, hands in the pockets of his jeans, knees dirty from kneeling. An uncertain expression crossed his face, but a little smile emerged for Franklin as he left. A vampire rescuing a stray dog. Franklin shook his head and made for his car.

On the way back, Franklin stopped at a twenty-four-hour grocery to pick up some bribes. Packaged turkey and dry kibble should do the trick. The store sold basic collars and leashes in their pet aisle, so he picked those up too, along with a plush squirrel. Maybe the dog would like a toy.

He pulled into the alley, headlights illuminating Gianni's lithe figure kneeling nimbly on the street, still beckoning the stray. Franklin got out of the car as Gianni stood and stretched.

"I should have known you'd drive a sports car."

Franklin shrugged. The old Mustang wasn't anything special, but he liked it. "Any luck?"

"No, she's scared of me. I can't get her to come any closer."

Franklin tore open the packaging and got out a slice of turkey. "Try this."

"Here, girl. You hungry? Come on." Gianni reached his arm toward the stray. Her ears perked, nose sniffing the air, but she didn't budge. "Maybe she doesn't like me. You try."

Franklin took the lunch meat and sat down, leaning back

against a building. He stretched out his legs and made himself relax. Then he took a bite of the turkey while the dog watched. "Mmm, it's good. I bet you're hungry. You want some? I'll share it with you." He took another bite.

Gianni observed from the other side of the alley, arms crossed over his chest. Franklin continued eating, plucking more turkey from the package. "Come on, get some. I know you want to." He clicked his tongue and kept his eyes downcast, not staring at the little dog directly.

The dog rose and took a tentative step forward. Franklin lay the turkey on the ground and pretended to ignore her. One cautious step at a time, she came, until she was close enough to gobble up the turkey and retreat.

"Good girl. That wasn't so hard. See? There's more." Franklin held the next slice at his side, waiting patiently. She took it from his hand. He risked a glance in her direction. She was a pretty thing, or she would be when she had a bath. Acorn brown fur going every which way, long floppy ears with curling tendrils, almond-shaped eyes. Definitely a spaniel mix.

"Gianni, come sit next to me. Bring the collar and leash."

The vampire did, but his presence scared the dog back behind the dumpster.

"She doesn't like me. Maybe I should leave."

"You probably smell like a predator. Their noses are thousands of times more sensitive than ours. Let her get used to you." Franklin took a slice of turkey and handed Gianni the rest. "Hold that." He gave his attention back to the dog. "Come on back. This is for you."

They sat together patiently, side by side on the grubby street, waiting for the stray to find her courage. "I always wanted a dog," Franklin said.

"Why didn't you have one?"

"My dad would never allow it. Too much of a distraction from training."

"That's sad."

Hunger won out, and the stray took the treat from Franklin.

"Now you hold some out for her."

Gianni stretched across Franklin's lap toward the dog, turkey in hand.

"Don't look straight at her. That's threatening for a dog. Ignore her and she'll come to you." They didn't have to wait long. The stray was probably starving. Soon enough, she was eating from Gianni's hand while Franklin scratched her chest and shoulders. She leaned into the touch.

Gianni steadily reached for the dog's chest with his free hand. He had to lean against Franklin to do it. Their fingers brushed as they petted her together. Side by side like this, working together to befriend a dog, remembering they were supposed to be enemies was hard. Easy to believe they could be more.

Franklin broke free from wandering thoughts. They had a task to accomplish if they wanted to lead her to safety. "Time for the hard part." Franklin slipped the collar over her head and latched the buckle. When she didn't seem to care, he clipped on the leash. "We got her. She must have been someone's dog. She's used to being collared."

Gianni frowned. "I wonder what happened."

They let her polish off the turkey before loading her into the car.

"Do you want to keep this dog?" Franklin asked.

"I can't. I live at the Farthing. There aren't any dogs."

"Vampires don't like dogs?"

"I guess not. Or maybe dogs don't like vampires." Gianni sighed and gazed over at Franklin, eyes sparkling and hopeful. "But you could keep her."

Franklin could keep her. Nothing was stopping him. But he hadn't planned on getting a dog. Maybe after Gianni left him, he would.

They loaded the dog into the car and drove to the shelter. A wire fence surrounded the building. They could tie her to it, and the staff would find her in the morning, but that might scare her.

"What if the shelter puts her down—" Gianni's eyes had grown watery.

"I'll make sure they don't."

"I'll wait with you as long as I can."

Franklin and Gianni's clothes were already dirty from the alley. They sat together right on the sidewalk, dog tied to the fence next to them, and waited for dawn. Gianni nudged him with his elbow.

"We could name her Spike, in keeping with the theme."

"What theme?"

"Buffy." Gianni paused, and when Franklin only stared at him, he added, "Seriously?"

"Seriously, what? I don't know what you're talking about most of the time."

"Buffy and Spike." Franklin's blank look must have prompted him on. "From the TV show? *Buffy the Vampire Slayer?*"

"Oh. I never watched the show. I wasn't allowed to watch TV."

"Jesus. Child abuse. That show is a classic. It should be required viewing for your lot."

"If you say so."

"I do. Buffy was the slayer, obviously. And Spike was the big bad vampire, but then he turned good for a while, then bad again, but he fell in love with Buffy so…"

Franklin settled in for several hours of teasing before Gianni had to leave to avoid sunrise. The dog seemed to take the situation in stride. She really was a good girl. Franklin thought Spike was a dumb name for a girl dog, or any dog, but if Gianni wanted it, he wouldn't argue.

The first rays of daylight teased the sky.

"I have to go," Gianni said, shoulders slumped. "Sorry to leave you waiting alone."

"I'm not alone. I have Spike." Franklin gave the dog a pat. "It'll just be a few more hours until they open."

"Still, I wish I could stay." Gianni turned to face him. "Thanks for looking out for her."

Franklin was about to say *no problem* when the vampire leaned in. Fingertips touched his jaw. He thought for sure he was about to be kissed, but at the last second Gianni dodged his lips, and the kiss landed on his cheek.

Adrenaline rushing through his veins, he watched the vampire trot away to wherever he slept during the day. Franklin touched his cheek.

9

MONSTER

Gianni

Tabea would understand if Gianni was in a hurry. He hated to snack and run but was eager for an update on Spike and couldn't dawdle. He'd tell her about the dog, and she'd get it. Surely she had better things to do anyway.

He'd nearly reached her place when that familiar tingle raised the hair on the back on his neck. It traveled the length of his spine and settled with a flutter in his gut. Gianni stamped down a flicker of poorly timed arousal. *The slayer.* But Gianni was nowhere near their familiar haunts. How did the man find him tonight?

He stopped in his tracks and scanned the dark street behind him. "Are you back to being a creeper, stalking me from the shadows? Where are you?"

Buffy turned the corner with both hands in the air. "I wasn't hiding. I just hadn't caught up with you yet."

"How did you find me?" Gianni scrunched his eyebrows together. "Did you plant a tracking device on me?"

"Hello to you, too."

"Right, yes. Hello. So, tracking device?"

"Would you believe I got lucky?"

"No."

The slayer shrugged. "Don't you want to know what happened with Spike?"

He let the matter drop in favor of news. "Is she okay?"

"She's perfectly fine. We're lucky they had room for her. She's in their intake now, which means a quarantine until they get her vaccinated and healthy. Then she'll be put up for adoption. They scanned her for a microchip, but she didn't have one. No one's called looking for a dog like her."

"Maybe she was abandoned."

"Maybe."

"She must be lonely."

"She's in good hands now. They'll find her a home."

Gianni wasn't completely satisfied, but he also couldn't have a dog. It was the best they could do. Unless... "Would you take her?"

Buffy tilted his head, eyes cast down. "I really can't."

"But you do want her?"

He nodded. "I've always wanted a dog. She's sweet. I think she's probably smart too. But what kind of life is this for a dog?" He gestured to the empty street with open palms.

"I don't know. It might be great. Walking around all night. Dogs love walking around."

"They're not nocturnal."

"Neither are you, really. You could give up the slayage. Not that you're doing much of it lately."

"I wish I could take her, but I don't have room in my life for a dog right now. Spike can do better."

A number of smartass replies danced on the tip of Gianni's tongue, but what came out was, "She'd be lucky to have you." He felt blood rush to his cheeks and couldn't meet Buffy's eyes.

"Anyway, you'd better leave me alone for a bit. I have an appointment. I can meet you somewhere later."

"An appointment?"

"Yes, nosy, and I need to go now. Where should I meet you?"

"The ballpark? One hour?"

"Okay, see you then."

Buffy nodded, and Gianni watched him leave before continuing. At least now he wouldn't be in such a hurry. And Spike was okay. Too bad Buffy couldn't keep her. Gianni had trouble resisting him as it was; with a little brown furry friend trotting after him, there'd be no winning that battle.

Tabea greeted him with a welcoming smile. "Come inside."

"Hey, Tabea, thank you." The house smelled good again, not like cooking this time, but as if she'd lit candles. It was a spicy and warm autumn scent, pumpkin seasoned something or other. They both sat on the couch. Gianni still wasn't sure how to do away with the small talk, and he didn't want to be rude. "How was your week?"

"Busy. I had a midterm and some writing to finish. This far into the semester is crunch time. I always end up behind." She moved her hair out of the way.

So hospitable. This was such a weird transaction; Gianni was grateful to her for making it simple. "How'd you do?" he asked to be polite, but he was already staring at her neck. The tingle down his spine he chalked up to anticipation.

"I got an A. Go ahead. I'm all set." She offered her throat.

Gianni took the back of her neck in his hand and leaned in. She met him in the middle. He closed his eyes and bit. Metallic warmth rushed over his tongue, into his stomach, and spread through his body like an embrace. The coppery sweetness flowed thick from her flesh. He fought back a moan.

A loud crash pounded into the room.

The floor shook as the door burst from its hinges. There was no time to gather himself as two powerful hands gripped his biceps, ripped him from Tabea, and flung him across the room. He landed hard, his lower back slamming into a side table. Blood spatter wet his face.

Tabea screamed, scrabbled backward off the couch, and put her back to the wall. She tore the shade off a lamp and brandished the base like a weapon. "What the fuck?"

Gianni was sprawled out on the floor, staring up at the slayer, who stood in the center of the room. He filled the space like a nightmare: fists clenched at his side, cheeks aflame, nostrils flared.

"Goddammit, Buffy, what the hell?"

"I can't let you kill her!" he roared.

"What the fuck do you think you saw? I wasn't going to hurt her." Gianni picked himself up off the floor, elbowed his way past Buffy, and went to soothe Tabea.

Her eyes darted back and forth between them. She was still holding the lamp in front of her.

"I know what I saw. You were drinking her blood." Fists clenching at his sides, the slayer appeared to barely hold back his strength.

"I'm a vampire. It's normal, or did you forget?" Gianni sniped. Then softer, to Tabea, "I'm sorry. He's a slayer, but I know him. It's okay—"

"It is *not* okay. And it is *not* normal," the slayer interrupted, fuming.

"Stop it. You're scaring my friend," Gianni said, lowering his voice. "There are none of us holy. We're all food for something, Buffy."

"Stop calling me that."

Gianni rounded on him. "Then tell me your name!"

They stared at each other, tension thick like cold molasses.

Tabea's death grip on the lamp didn't falter.

"You should leave. I need to heal the punctures, and I don't want you ripping me off her this time. She could have been hurt."

"She *was* being hurt! You're a monster, just like the others. I don't know why they think you're different."

"I'm the monster here? Look what you did." Gianni gestured to Tabea. Her eyes were wide and her heartbeat elevated. Blood ran down her neck, ruining her lovely yellow blouse.

"I'm not the one that fucking bit her like a rabid animal!"

"Get out," Gianni said, voice dangerously calm so as not to upset Tabea further.

Their eyes met. Buffy looked like he'd refuse, like there was more he had to say. He turned his attention to Tabea.

"Are you okay?"

"Get out," she echoed.

The slayer gaped in disbelief, as if he couldn't understand what he'd heard. For a heartbeat, nobody moved. Then Gianni watched, frozen in place, as the slayer stormed through the empty doorframe and into the night.

Well, that could have gone better.

When he was certain Buffy wasn't lingering, he turned back to Tabea. She held her neck with one hand and the lamp with the other. She looked calmer now, but still traumatized.

Gianni took a deep breath, gently removed the lamp from her grasp, and set it back on the table. "I am so sorry."

"Who was that lunatic?"

"I thought I knew, but I guess I don't. I've sort of been seeing him. He won't hurt you, though, I swear. He thought he was protecting you from me."

She tilted her head. "He's a vampire hunter?"

"Yeah."

"Buffy?"

"He won't tell me his real name," Gianni admitted sadly.

"Why are you hanging out with a vampire hunter? Do you have a death wish?"

"Maybe. I'm starting to think so. Let me take care of this for you."

She removed her hand. Carefully, Gianni bent to her throat and licked the punctures closed. He lapped the drying blood from her skin and retreated. "Your shirt, it's ruined. I'm sorry."

"Stop apologizing. It's not your fault."

"It is, though. I get this feeling when he's around, like a fluttering just under my skin. It's hard to explain. I felt it, but I thought I was just hungry. I ignored it."

"Well, I'm all right now. Come on. Let's get cleaned up." She led him to a bathroom and ran water into the sink.

"I'll get the council to send money for the repairs. Oh, god. How am I going to explain this?"

"Yeah, how are you going to do that?" Tabea soaked a cloth and reached for his face. Gianni watched their reflections in the mirror—pale, wide-eyed. They both looked shell-shocked. She washed the blood spatter off his lips and cheeks while he pondered what lie the council might believe about a slayer interrupting a blood donation and leaving without a kill.

"On second thought, let me pay you directly."

"Whatever. My boyfriend will fix the door." She took his chin and turned him from the mirror to face her. He met her gaze, her dark brown eyes serious. "You know you need to stop seeing that guy, right?"

"He really isn't that bad."

"You don't even know his name." She gave him a look. "The hunters are so prejudiced against vampires they don't know an ass from an elbow. He's been indoctrinated, Gianni. He'll never be able to get to know the real you. You're risking your life every time you see him."

Unshed tears stung his eyes. She was right.

"Oh no. You've got it bad."

Gianni squinted, scrunched up his nose to stop the tears from falling. "Maybe a little."

"Just be careful. You seem nice. You can do better."

"Believe me when I tell you I can't. I'll bring money for the door. Is tomorrow night okay? I should go."

"You're chasing after him?"

Gianni let his silence speak for itself.

"Tomorrow's fine. Don't get dead."

"Right. No dying. Check."

Gianni left Tabea alone to change her clothes and call her boyfriend about the door. He went straight to the ballpark, but the slayer wasn't there.

Gianni sat on their bench and waited. He stayed all night in the cold, even when he'd lost hope the man would show. The tingle on the back of his neck never came.

Loneliness set in with the morning fog, hazy and dense.

***

Franklin

"I fucked up. He hates me now," Franklin told Darrow, the two of them alone in the chief's office. He hadn't meant to be so honest, but the chief had caught him off-guard, asking after his plans, and it just came out.

"What do you mean? What happened?"

Franklin gave a truthful, if abbreviated, version of the story. "He was furious. The woman was terrified. She was actually afraid of *me* and not him. He won't forgive me for this."

"You don't know that," Darrow said. "Let's see if it's salvageable before we move forward with the live capture. Give him some time to cool off, say you're sorry, and then ask after the girl."

For a moment, Franklin had almost forgotten about the live capture. What was he doing? He didn't want Gianni to end up as a test subject in the Scourge's lab. He should never have told

Darrow the truth. He stood straighter and squared his shoulders.

"You're right. I can fix this."

"That's the spirit. He wants to know your name. It couldn't hurt to give some ground."

"But…" Franklin had been taught names held power among the undead, that he should never reveal his. "Is that safe? Are you sure?"

"You don't have to give him your real name. Call yourself anything. He'll never know the difference."

That simple solution hadn't occurred to him. Now it was obvious. Gianni would be mad if he found out, but he never had to know. Maybe it would work, and they could go back to the way things were. Later, once Franklin convinced him to leave, they wouldn't see each other again.

Rubbing his neck, Franklin collected his thoughts. Gianni had looked every bit the predator as he was leaning over that girl—blood donor—whatever she was. Franklin should have been angry at the sight, but the truth was jealousy had risen up inside him like vomit. The emotion shocked him. He hadn't held back, throwing Gianni like a rag doll. The vampire would have bruises. Bruises Franklin had caused. The thought made him ill. Gianni shouldn't forgive him, but he'd have to convince the vampire to listen somehow, for his own good.

Perhaps giving him a name would do it.

If Franklin could find him.

10

NEW FRIENDS

Gianni

If Buffy didn't want to see him anymore, that was fine. It was time Gianni got over himself and made new friends. Tabea was right. He was courting danger, and for what? Buffy's tolerance? Discerning his endgame was impossible, but it probably wasn't what Gianni wanted. The more time they spent together, the more he longed for Buffy to be his companion, to be his lover. Since that obviously wasn't going to happen, he'd cut his losses and move on.

With that in mind, he made himself pretty, but not too pretty because he didn't want to outshine any of the women he planned to befriend. He'd noticed a group of younger vampires who didn't laugh or sneer at him. With any luck, he'd talk his way into whatever their plans were for the night. He had to get out and get his mind off the slayer.

Hayleigh was the loudest of the group, the most popular and confident, and thus the one Gianni needed to win over to earn an invitation. He marched straight to her suite, entirely prepared to beg.

She smiled at finding him outside her door. "Gianni, this is a surprise." She tucked a lock of golden blonde hair behind her ear. "Come in. What brings you here?"

Maybe he wouldn't need to grovel after all. Honesty was the best policy, right? It couldn't make things any worse. Plus, she looked friendly, her oval face lit with curiosity and a welcoming grin on her lips. She wasn't dressed to go out, but it was still early. There was time to convince her.

"I'm crazy bored, Hayleigh. I've got to make some friends before I die old and alone. Everyone hates me, and I can't even have a dog. Can I hang out with you?" There. The truth. Gianni waited with bated breath.

Hayleigh gave a warm belly laugh, her smile revealing the top row of her white teeth and glistening fangs. She swept her arm toward the living room and stood back to let him pass. "For Christ's sake, sit down. Of course you can hang out with me. Why do you even want a dog?"

Gianni released a breath. Relief filled his chest. He could kiss her. "Thanks. That was easier than I thought it would be. I don't really know if I want a dog. It's complicated."

Her place was decorated in jewel tones with rich fabrics and textures, and her collection of throw pillows rivaled his. He wanted to walk around her sitting room and touch things. He took a seat on a ruby red leather sofa. "Will your friends mind too much, do you think?" He brushed his fingers over a satin tassel. "I seem to be the laughingstock around here."

"Jess and Avery? Are you kidding? They don't give a shit what the others think, but I can't promise they won't have questions."

"Right, questions." Gianni was resigned. This part was unavoidable.

"I have a few myself. The rumors about you are wild."

"Probably all true, though I don't know what people are saying. I was an idiot. Lots of bad decisions."

Hayleigh sat in the chair opposite and leaned back, crossing her legs.

Gianni could see she was burning to ask something, but politeness held her back. "Go ahead. Hit me with your questions. I can take it."

She leaned in. "Did you really think the sovereign of Philly would change you? That's, like, unheard of."

"I'm afraid so. Hook, line, and sinker. An ancient changed him, so I thought I could get him to break with tradition as well. It would be nice to start my undead life so powerful. Was hoping to be promoted from bedwarmer to co-sovereign. I never claimed to be smart."

"Jesus. And all those things you did for him? Did he really make you sleep with visiting sovereigns?"

"Also true." Gianni gave a little shrug. *What can you do?* "Seemed worth it at the time."

"We all make mistakes," she offered, mirroring his shrug.

"We don't all let assholes livestream them. That's exclusive to me." The sovereign of Chicago had an exhibitionist streak, and Gianni hadn't felt like he could say no. It would be a long time before he lived that one down. He cringed, wondering if she'd watched it.

"He was an asshole for pushing you to do those things in the first place, but you win the prize for best-worst-mistake. I can't compete with that." She leaned farther into the couch and tucked her feet up.

Gianni laughed. "I don't suggest you try. The fallout sucks."

"Once, I pretended to be a student at a university to seduce a professor I fancied. I thought myself quite racy at the time. He was delicious." Hayleigh grinned and licked her lips. "I was so into him, I told him what I was, but he freaked out. I had to compel him to forget."

"His loss."

"You're sweet. You know, I've never met a living vampire before."

Gianni leapt at the subject change. He didn't want to relive his worst moments or remind her of hers. "There aren't very many of us." Currently, there were less than a hundred in the whole world, dwindling down to only a few familial lines. So few that reproduction had to follow a strict plan to avoid inbreeding.

"Are you eager to be changed?"

Gianni sat back. He'd been trying not to think about this. "Not anymore. I used to be eager to be a turned vampire, but now I don't know. Would you go back if you could?"

"To being human? No way!" Hayleigh shook her head. "Not for a million dollars. This is better. It might be hard for you to understand—you've never been human. They're so fragile. Even a living vampire is stronger than a human."

"Stronger, faster, less impervious to disease and such, but we're still fragile compared to undead vampires. I used to worry more about what could happen if I ever really got hurt, but I don't so much now."

"Why not?" Hayleigh asked.

"Well, being away from Oswald helped. No one takes pleasure in hurting me lately, so there's that."

Hayleigh leaned forward in her seat, locking her eyes with his. "I'm glad you got away."

Gianni smiled. "Thanks, me too. Can I ask how old you are? Or is that rude?"

"It's probably rude." She laughed. "But I think I owe you one. I'm thirty-five. I was made a vampire six years ago. Jess and Avery are similar. How old are you?"

"Twenty-six. But I feel eighty."

"Well, you're as dramatic as everyone says you are."

"Guilty." Gianni grinned.

"Let me text the others. You're bored, right? We'll take you out. What do you want to do?"

"Seriously? You're a queen." Gianni clapped his hands together. "Dancing. Can we go dancing?"

"Of course."

"The human club though, do you know it? The Mint Lounge? I can't deal with any vampire bullshit tonight."

"The Mint Lounge it is."

Jess and Avery turned out to be just as nice, if not quite as outspoken, as Hayleigh. Avery brought her partner, Bryson, giving Gianni so much company he almost felt popular. Why hadn't he done this before? Oswald had made him forget all his social skills. He used to be good at making friends. Maybe he still was. Now that he was dancing with this new group and anyone who cared to join them, it wasn't so hard. Just be nice and maybe shake your ass a little. Simple.

The others ordered cocktails, and Gianni drank them one by one when the bartender wasn't looking. He was the only one who could. They were amused by his party trick, a vampire who could drink something other than blood, as Buffy had been.

Damnit.

He swore he wasn't going to think about the slayer.

A few more drinks and he made good on that promise. Gianni wasn't thinking about anything. He danced with Bryson. He danced with strangers. He danced with Hayleigh. He danced by himself. The music was loud and his vision pleasantly fuzzy. Gianni forgot his troubles and let himself pulse to the beat.

They closed the club down. It was two a.m. when they left, pouring out onto the street in a fit of giggles. The crisp night air refreshed his senses. Being part of a group again felt marvelous, exactly what he needed.

Until.

It started with that fucking tingle. The hairs on the back of his neck prickled. A shiver coursed down his spine.

Buffy.

Gianni cast his eyes quickly over their surroundings, searching. Across the street, partially hidden by shadows under the awning of a pawn shop, stood his slayer.

He looked…heartbroken.

Gianni sobered up in an instant, narrowing his gaze and focusing. He hadn't imagined it—Buffy looked sad. Gianni wanted to go to him, but he forced himself to play it cool. These vampires could not know about the slayer. Four on one were terrible odds.

If they saw him, Buffy was as good as dead.

Gianni tore his gaze from Buffy and turned his attention back to the others. He took Hayleigh's hand, kissed it, and practically dragged her down the street.

"Let's get out of here."

Franklin

Gianni looked happy.

And drunk, definitely drunk.

Franklin watched him stumble out of the club, a pack of vampires in tow. Five vampires in a group were lethal. A lone slayer had no business hanging out across the street from a pack that size, but there he stood, frozen in place, watching Gianni. Always watching Gianni.

The vampire saw him. Of course he did. Somehow, Gianni knew when Franklin was watching. Their eyes met, and Franklin wanted to call out to him, but he couldn't. That would be suicide. So he stared with jealousy churning in his gut as Gianni led the jovial group away.

He had no right to be jealous. This was his fault. When he saw those fangs, he overreacted. What the Scourge thought about vampires didn't matter; he knew Gianni better than that.

Long after he'd watched Gianni walk away, hand in hand with another vampire, Franklin left his spot on the street. He was headed back toward the Foundry when Hutch caught up to him. The last thing he needed was to speak to another slayer. He wanted to be alone with his thoughts.

"What's up? How's it going with your freaky boyfriend?"

Franklin only glared.

Hutch laughed. "Sorry, bro. You could have done worse. At least he's hot. For a dude."

Franklin still had nothing to say. Too bad he couldn't slay a fellow hunter.

"Oh, come on, lighten up. I'm just kidding. Seriously, how's it going?"

"It's not. He's out with a bunch of other vampires tonight."

"Bummer." Hutch bumped their shoulders, like they were friends. It was weird and made Franklin suspicious.

"You can hunt with me if you want," Hutch said. "I thought I'd scope out the ghetto, look for some easy pickings."

"Thanks, but no. Got a mission of my own tonight."

"Whatever, dude. Keep me in mind for the live capture team, okay? I want in."

"Okay." *Yeah, right.* He'd warn Gianni before it came to that. If he thought he could still go through with it, he was kidding himself.

Hutch rushed off, and Franklin returned to the quiet of his rooms in the Foundry, opened the giant tome of vampire history he'd been studying, and got to work. Knowledge was power, and if he couldn't hand Gianni over to the Scourge, maybe he could learn enough from him to make a worthwhile addition to the history books.

There wasn't much written on living vampires—a few legends, most considered myths by the Scourge's top scholars. He'd read them all cover to cover. A line of vampires descended through the ages, not undead, but not human. Mortal until some ordinary vampire changed them. Then it was believed they became just like the others. Little else was known of the species. They were fertile, obviously, or there wouldn't be descendants. Undead vampires were sterile and family lines drawn from sire to fledging, not father to son.

Franklin had studied this before, but never with an actual live sample in mind. Gianni brought the old text to life. The vampire was in the forefront of his mind as he read each passage. Finally, he stumbled onto something with potential.

In every case, the living vampire is fiercely protected by his undead cohorts. Thus, no specimen has been acquired for closer study. It is theorized the living vampire is akin to royalty, in which case they very well may be the ruling class of vampire society. There is yet no evidence to support this claim.

A secondary hypothesis exists, though we may never have the means to test it. It could be that the living vampire finds himself so heavily guarded due to the powerful nature of his blood. It is known that the blood of a common undead vampire has tremendous medicinal value. Small infusions are capable of healing minor wounds, large infusions heal even the most catastrophic damage, and total transfusion smites mortality itself to the point of undeath.

If the blood of the undead can work such miracles, what possibilities exist of the blood of the living?

Franklin stopped reading. He didn't know why Gianni was never protected by other vampires, but the text had been written a thousand years ago. Things may have changed. Even so, surely this was why the Scourge desperately wanted a living test subject. Why they wanted Gianni.

What if Franklin could get the information another way? What if he simply asked? Would Gianni tell him? Probably not now, not with Gianni angry with him, but if he apologized… If he could win the vampire over and get this much information out of him, he could warn Gianni away and tell the Scourge what he'd learned.

He'd save the vampire and the mission, probably avoid a demotion. Especially if he could get a sample of blood. Gianni would never agree, but Franklin wouldn't ask permission. It was the only way. Franklin added a small glass vial next to the knife in the pocket of his cargo pants. Gianni would be angry, but he wouldn't try to kill him.

Probably.

11

BRISTOL SPRINGS

Gianni

At the springs. G

ianni left the three-word note under a rock on their park bench and headed for the water. In theory, he knew Bristol Springs was named for actual springs, but going there hadn't occurred to him. Hayleigh encouraged him to visit. She said the area was beautiful and the springs themselves were warm pools of crystal clear water. She wasn't wrong; the springs were enchanting.

He'd slipped between granite boulders and through fragrant evergreens on the well-worn quarter-mile path to the water. Once there, the view opened up to a panorama of swimming holes: some large enough for groups; others built into the rock itself, private cedar tubs for only one or two people. Gianni dipped his fingers into the pond to discover it was indeed warm as bath water, and he had the whole place to himself. He immediately began taking off his clothes.

Of course, he hoped Buffy would come. In the back of his

mind, he knew he should probably stay dressed. They had a serious conversation ahead of them if they were going to remain friends, or whatever they were, but the water's allure was too tempting. He had to get in. Buffy would deal—if he bothered to show up.

Gianni stripped down to nothing and eased himself into the healing warmth of one of the larger pools. Oh gods, it was luxurious, the temperature in perfect contrast to the crisp night air. Gianni pushed away from the shore and ducked his head under, wetting his hair. He swam to the center of the pool and floated on his back, eyes closed, listening.

Sound had an eerie quality to it underwater, a soothing kind of sensory deprivation calming his nerves and easing the tension in his shoulders. No wonder people flocked to this place. No wonder a town had sprung up around this majesty. He was only sorry visiting took him this long.

The tingling sensation alerting him to the slayer's presence apparently worked fine through water. Gianni kept his eyes closed and pretended not to notice. Some part of him wondered how long Buffy would look before he said anything.

That answer was a really long fucking time.

Gianni got tired of waiting. He opened his eyes and caught Buffy staring. The man looked away immediately. His cheeks turned pink, and he shoved his hands into his pockets, backing away.

"Uh, sorry."

Gianni swam over to the manmade rail in the deep side of the pool so his body would be mostly hidden by the water. "I'm not bothered. You're cute when you're embarrassed. Come over."

"You're not mad at me?" He approached, posture wary.

"Mad at you for what? Watching me swim naked or terrorizing my friend?"

"The second one. You wanted me to see you naked." Still projecting caution, Buffy stood over him by the pool's ledge.

"I'm a little mad, but it was partially my fault. Sit down."

Buffy sat, folding his long limbs awkwardly on the large slab of granite.

Gianni propped his elbows up on the wooden pool rail between them.

"Is she really your friend? The blood donor?"

Gianni nodded. "Her name is Tabea. We're friendly. I've only known her a week. I'd like to be her friend. Are you going to apologize?"

"I'm working my way up to it. Are you planning on forgiving me?"

"Depends on the apology, I guess. Better make it good." Gianni let his body float up in the water, kicking his feet behind him. Buffy's eyes were drawn to the motion—and his ass.

"I'm sorry. I overreacted."

"Better than that."

"I'm sorry I overreacted and scared your friend."

"Now say it without staring at my ass."

Buffy returned his gaze to Gianni's face. "Sorry."

"I forgive you. Don't do it again."

"Scare your friend or stare at your ass?"

"Don't scare my friend. If you want to see my ass, you only have to ask."

Buffy nodded, mouth closed, and kept his eyes on Gianni's face. The blush crept back onto his cheeks.

"I didn't know if you still wanted to see me. After you saw… what you saw," Gianni gave voice to his doubts.

"I did. I do." Buffy dipped his fingers into the pool.

"I'm glad. You seemed pretty angry." Gianni watched the slayer's hand swirling the water next to him. It was easier than catching his gaze.

"I was." He stilled. "At the time. Later, I realized it wasn't your fault. You've never hidden the fact that you're a vampire. It was just hard to be confronted with the reality of it. Seeing you…feed."

"I did tell you to leave. Before."

"You did." Buffy tilted his head in acknowledgment. "I should've listened."

"I waited for you in the park, but you never came."

"I'm sorry. I didn't think you'd want to see me."

Gianni glanced up. The slayer looked sincere. "I saw you at the club."

"I know. You were with a bunch of vampires. You were drunk."

"I was. You looked sad."

Buffy cast his eyes downward. Gianni took pity on him. Time to lighten the mood.

"Help me up." Gianni stretched out a hand.

"You're naked."

Gianni winked. "You're welcome. Help me up."

Buffy stood and offered his hand to pull him from the pool, but as soon as Gianni took hold, he yanked, throwing the slayer off balance and tipping him into the water. Buffy splashed and flailed, righting himself as he came up sputtering. Gianni lost himself in a fit of giggles.

"Now I bet you wish you were naked too." He continued to laugh. Buffy looked even more adorable soaking wet, his hair in his eyes, treading water fully clothed. His shirt clung to the muscles of his shoulders above the surface, and the fabric in the water floated loosely over his frame. Gianni was captivated. For a second he thought Buffy might be angry with him, but then a smile spread across his face, and he joined in the laughter.

"You little shit." Buffy swiped the hair out of his eyes.

Gianni pushed him to the side of the pool and pinned him there with his body, arms around his shoulders. They stopped laughing. He was close enough to breathe Buffy's air. The slayer was warm against him, wet clothes tangled between them. Buffy was staring at his mouth.

"What's your name?"

The slayer's gaze traveled from his lips to his eyes. He hesitated for so long, Gianni thought he would be denied once more. Then, finally, and in a rush, he whispered, "Richard," before crushing their lips together.

Richard.

His name was Richard.

Butterflies chased each other deep in Gianni's stomach as he leaned into the kiss, opening his mouth for Richard's tongue. Everything was warm and wet. Gianni closed his eyes to concentrate on the feel of him. The taste. Sweet and rich like cream over fruit. Richard kissed as if he was starving, and Gianni wanted to feed him.

Richard wrapped his arms around Gianni's waist, pulling him in tight. Gianni massaged his scalp, feeling him everywhere: against his chest, in his mouth, under his hands. Richard made a sound against Gianni's lips, a whimper really, and it went straight to his dick. Returning it hungrily, he poured himself into the kiss.

When they broke apart, it was to look into each other's eyes anew. Richard had stunning emerald green eyes, and he so rarely let eye contact linger for more than a heartbeat. Gianni had to kiss him again. Once, twice, and another for good measure, all while coming back over and over to those eyes.

He'd grown hard and pressed himself against Richard's hip. The slayer was in the same state. Undoing his pants, getting a hand on his erection, and working him until he came would be so easy. What sound would he make against Gianni's mouth then? But he held himself back. Their first time should be in a bed. Dry. Not a quick handjob in the hot springs. Though ravishing him in this warm pool was tempting.

"You're good at this." Gianni dragged himself from Richard's mouth long enough to speak.

"So are you." Richard's emerald gaze was intense.

Gianni delighted in it.

"Yeah, well, I know *I'm* good at it. You're more of a surprise." Gianni kissed him again, but Richard pulled back, smiling.

"What's that supposed to mean?"

"You're so uptight. I never pegged you for a good kisser."

"Mm, not uptight," Richard mumbled against Gianni's lips.

"Stop talking. Stick to what you're good at."

Gianni felt Richard's grip on him tighten, and the slayer pushed from the wall, reversing their positions and pinning Gianni to the ledge. Oh, and that was nice. Their cocks lined up perfectly. He flexed his hips into Richard's, tipped his head back, and moaned. They rocked together.

"Jesus." Gianni stopped to catch his breath. "You feel good."

"Yeah, you do too."

"Richard," Gianni tested the name on his lips. "Kiss me again."

Gianni couldn't get enough. Richard's mouth was made for him. He sucked on his tongue and fought the urge to bite down. How could he convince the slayer to let him have a taste? His blood would be divine, but this wasn't the time to find out. He broke from the kiss and made himself take a deep breath. If he wanted to wait for a bed, he had to calm down.

Now he had a problem. Richard's clothes were soaked, and it was far too chilly for him to stay in them outside of the pool.

Gianni sighed. "It's cold out tonight."

"It is."

"I probably shouldn't have gotten your clothes all wet, but it was worth it. I'm not going to apologize." Gianni reached into one of Richard's pockets. A pocket knife, a cylinder…no keys.

Richard stiffened. "I wouldn't want you to."

"Good." He reached into another and found what he was after. Keys. "Then you'll tell me where you've parked your car."

"Oh." Richard relaxed.

Gianni watched as reality dawned across Richard's face in the form of a shadow of disappointment. They weren't going to continue their frottage in the hot springs. Gianni would fetch his car so he wouldn't have to walk across the city soaking wet.

"You know the public lot across from the courthouse? It's there."

"I'll go get it." Gianni gave him a quick peck and climbed out of the water.

"I guess I'll just be here."

"Doing what, exactly?" Gianni smirked.

"Let's not talk about it."

"Hey, Richard?"

"Yeah?"

"Feel free to stare at my ass." Gianni turned his back to Richard and got dressed.

Slowly.

Franklin

On the one hand, he was an absolute piece of shit for giving Gianni a fake name, and he felt like a dick. On the other hand, he'd wrangled enough courage to kiss the vampire, and it was the best kiss of his life. The high still lingered, a pleasant buzz as he floated through the Foundry's halls. The combination left him spinning.

Gianni had fetched his car and driven it back to the springs. Somewhere along the way, he'd picked up towels and a pair of sweatpants so Franklin wouldn't have to get his seat wet. For all the sass coming from his mouth, Gianni's was a sweet and loving soul.

The more he thought about it, the more he wished he'd told Gianni his real name. He'd blown it, and there was no way to explain without making Gianni angry. Possibly furious. The risk wasn't worth it. He'd have to live with *Richard,* and with any luck, the vampire would never know.

Although he didn't want that either. Franklin was beginning to imagine a future with Gianni: cuddling on the couch; conversations until the wee hours of the morning; maybe a dog to keep them company… Such a thing wasn't possible. Franklin could only save him from the Scourge. He couldn't have him for himself. But he was torn. He wanted as much time with Gianni as possible before spilling his guts and dealing with the aftermath. The vampire's anger seemed inevitable—might as well delay it.

Franklin had to stop at his room for fresh clothes before he made his way to Darrow's office. The closer he got to Gianni, the more awkward these meetings had become.

"Lieutenant," Darrow greeted.

"Chief," Franklin began. He told Darrow about the note waiting for him at the park and of seeing Gianni at the hot springs. He left out the swimming, the kissing, and the complete lack of clothes on the part of the vampire. Darrow only wanted to know they were back on track. He didn't need the particulars.

"So giving him a name worked wonders, did it?" Darrow radiated *I told you so* as he leaned casually back in his chair, a grin on his face.

"Yes, that was a good call," Franklin admitted. "Thanks for the tip."

"You're welcome. Keep up the good work."

Darrow dismissed him, and Franklin went back to his quarters. He discarded the barely worn clothes and picked up the sweatpants Gianni had bought him. He climbed into the thick, soft cotton and untucked his sheets. Before waking to check on Spike, he'd get a few hours of sleep. Franklin wanted to know if their dog had settled in all right or maybe had been adopted already.

Sleep didn't come easily. Not with those divine kisses playing on repeat in his mind. Gianni had been eager in his arms, his weight against Franklin's chest light as they floated in the water. Smooth, supple skin beneath his fingertips, flesh warm in his palms, and Gianni's lips hot against his own. It wasn't different because Gianni was a man or because he was a vampire. It was different because he was *Gianni*—a forbidden flighty creature, both soft and sharp and somehow interested in Franklin.

He was ashamed of himself for all the lying. Gianni would see it as a betrayal, but was it? Franklin was going to keep him safe; he wouldn't turn him over to the Scourge. He was trying to help.

Bullshit. You're hurting him, and he doesn't even know yet. Franklin's sleep was restless, his mind divided and his body *wanting.*

FIRST BLOOD

Franklin

eople were still enjoying the park, kicking around soccer balls, jogging, getting some fresh air before bed. It was early yet, the last rays of sun streaking in horizontal lines, highlighting the autumn leaf show. Franklin walked along the perimeter, circling the ballfields in an endless loop, leaves crunching under his feet. Gianni would meet him at dusk. Until then, he fought not to let his nerves get the better of him.

He shouldn't have been nervous. Kissing Gianni had been easy. Simple as breathing. Franklin both wanted to do it again and was reluctant to dig the hole deeper. Climbing out from this mess after Gianni left would be a nightmare. If he was lucky, the Scourge would never know of his betrayal, but the rebound would be brutal.

After much consideration, Franklin decided he would apologize and tell Gianni his real name. Tonight. Before he could change his mind. If the vampire was mad, Franklin would just have to earn his forgiveness while they still had time.

As darkness set in, the other park-goers trickled out.

Franklin scanned the fields repeatedly until he caught Gianni approaching from the far entrance. He could go to him; he wanted to, but instead he waited, savoring the view.

Gianni had a spring in his step, walking with an eager bounce that was almost a trot. *Is that for me?* It was hard to believe. He wore tight black pants and a flowing top of peach fabric draping nearly to his knees. His dark hair was swept back, revealing his lovely oval face, animated with excitement and a wide smile for Franklin.

Franklin found himself smiling in return. Nerves replaced with pleasant anticipation, he opened his arms, and Gianni stepped into them. They fit together seamlessly, Gianni's face against his neck, the vampire placing little kisses along his throat. That should have worried him, but it didn't. Besides, it felt nice.

Gianni leaned back to make room for a kiss, and Franklin was happy to indulge him. Their lips met, warm and sweet. Franklin held Gianni close, hands tight against his lower back. He forgot to breathe.

Gianni giggled into his mouth and turned his head. "Air, Richard. We need air."

Hearing the stupid false name, Franklin deflated. He almost preferred Buffy. He would fix this; he just needed to find the right words. Franklin released Gianni from his grip and stood back to admire him. The vampire's lips were reddened and wet from kissing. Did his own mouth look like that? It wouldn't be nearly as flattering on him as it was on Gianni's perfect pout.

"Have I stunned you into silence?" Gianni grinned.

"You often do."

"You could tell me I look pretty."

"You always look pretty."

Gianni's smile widened. "Maybe you don't need my help after all, charmer." He linked their elbows, and together they walked toward town.

"I checked on Spike today." Franklin began with something easy before his big admission.

Gianni's face lit up. "How is she?"

"She was glad to see me. No one has called the shelter looking for her, so she's been put up for adoption."

"I hope someone nice wants her."

"Me too," Franklin agreed. Her ears had been droopy until she'd spotted him and perked up, wagging her tail. Leaving her there had been hard.

"I love these late night strolls with you." Gianni gave his elbow a squeeze. "You know, I never used to spend this much time outside."

"Why not?" Franklin watched as the pleasant expression on Gianni's face turned melancholy.

"Back in Philly, I was a different person. Greedy. Overly ambitious. I thought..." Gianni trailed off, staring off into the distance.

Franklin waited, a bit concerned by the shift in Gianni's mood.

When Gianni began again, he sounded more confident. "I thought status was more important than anything. It's all I cared about. I spent most of my energy struggling to improve mine, which meant courting and placating other vampires in society. Indoors. Often underground. I'd forgotten how nice fresh air is."

Franklin spent hours outside every single night. He couldn't imagine being cooped up indoors. Did Gianni want him to ask about his time in Philly? Would he rather not discuss it? Why was knowing what to say around him so difficult? It should have been easier now, but it wasn't.

Gianni filled the silence for them. "You wouldn't know about that sort of pandering, would you? There's nothing fake about you, Richard."

A sinking feeling took hold of his gut. Guilt was a heavy thing.

He was about to come clean and tell Gianni everything when they heard a scream followed by the sounds of a struggle in the distance. With a brief glance at each other, Gianni released his arm, and they ran toward the noise. Gianni flew ahead of him, and Franklin raced to keep up.

Another scream followed by a grunt came from a side street. Franklin rounded the corner to see Hutch facing off with a female vampire: long blonde hair, maybe five-foot-eight, not prepared for a fight, no weapon. She looked terrified. Hutch was full of glee. He had the advantage. She was already bleeding heavily from a stab wound in her left shoulder.

"Hayleigh!" Gianni cried, dashing directly into the middle of the fight, blocking her from Hutch.

Fuck.

That was the last thing he needed. As Hutch lunged for Gianni, Franklin ran into the fray.

Gianni dodged the silver knife, ducking low and swinging around to kick Hutch's legs out from under him.

The female vampire backed up but didn't flee. *Why?* Because they knew each other? Franklin took a closer look. Yes. This was the vampire from the dance club.

Hutch stumbled. Off balance, he struck out with the knife again. Franklin grabbed him around the middle and struggled to pull him back. It wasn't the most elegant end to a fight, but technique had no place in a street brawl.

Gianni stood braced for the offensive but waited, watching Franklin.

Franklin spun Hutch, putting his own back to the middle of the fight, and casting Hutch out of it. He shoved the other hunter forward, away from the action.

Pain flared sharp as razors in Franklin's neck. The female

was on him. He let out a roar, hands flailing to grab at her hair or take out an eye.

"Hayleigh, no!" Gianni yelled.

Her talons dug into his biceps, her teeth lodged in his neck.

Franklin tried to elbow her, but she was torn off him before he could swing his arm. He spun to see her caged and furious, trapped in Gianni's arms.

"What the hell?" she gasped out. "I had him. You get the other one!" She writhed in Gianni's grip, but he didn't let her go. He was saying something to her, but Franklin couldn't listen. It was time to get rid of Hutch. The hunter should have known better than to attack Gianni. What the fuck was he thinking?

"Get out of here," he ordered.

Hutch glared at him, duty warring with bloodlust in his eyes. Hutch knew about Franklin's assignment, but apparently he didn't care. "Let's kill her and take him. There's two of us—we can handle it."

Gianni shuttled Hayleigh further away, the two of them talking in fast whispers.

"That isn't the plan, and you know it. Go, while they're distracted."

Hutch still didn't move. "Afraid I'll hurt your little boyfriend?"

"Touch him, and I'll kill you." It came out of Franklin's mouth without hesitation.

Hutch tilted his head. "You're threatening me?"

"Yes."

"Over a vampire." It wasn't a question. Hutch shook his head, then motioned to Franklin's neck. "You're bleeding."

Franklin knew he was injured. He was beginning to feel lightheaded, but he needed Hutch to leave before he could give his wounds any attention.

"Hutch, clear out of here, or it'll be three against one."

Franklin siding with the vampires was sure to get the hunter to leave.

Hutch glared at him, eyes narrowed, still breathing heavily. "You're going to regret this." He stalked away.

Stumbling, Franklin spun to see the woman leaving in the other direction. He brought his hand to his neck and covered the stinging wound. His shirt was soaked with blood. She'd torn a large bite from his flesh. Spots danced in his vision. He started to collapse, but Gianni caught him. He lowered them carefully to the ground.

"Richard…" The vampire sighed the stupid fake name and removed Franklin's hand from the wound for his inspection. "This is bad."

Franklin knew as much. He could die here. His vision began to blur. He let Gianni prop him up, leaning against him.

"You have to let me help you," Gianni said, forcing eye contact. "We have to be quick. Hayleigh will have called for backup. They'll be here soon."

Franklin was having trouble understanding what he meant. He lost himself in the hazel gaze. Had Gianni been hurt in the shuffle? The vampire looked worried, not injured. "You okay?"

"I'm fine, but you're not. Be still." Gianni lowered his mouth to Franklin's throat and closed it over the wound. His tongue lapped at the sore flesh, and Franklin flinched. It hurt, but he was too weak to free himself. Before long, it stopped. Gianni made shushing noises and whispered into his ear, "You've lost too much blood. You need to drink from me."

"No." Franklin cringed at the thought, turning his face away.

Gianni took his chin in hand and moved him back. Franklin was so weak, he could offer no resistance. Their eyes locked, green on hazel.

"We don't have time to argue." Gianni's voice sounded more serious than usual. Franklin didn't like it. Where were the jokes?

"This isn't a request. I need you to drink. I'd rather you did it on your own, but I'll make you if I have to."

Franklin felt a tingling sensation at the base of his skull. As quickly as it came, it faded away. Gianni would use his power to compel him. The thought made him furious.

A tiny voice in the back of his mind whispered, *This is your chance to get the sample.* Through the haze of blood loss, Franklin fought to cling to rational thought and reached into his pocket for the glass vial.

As Franklin watched in horror, Gianni bit deeply into his own wrist. This was really happening. The wrist came away from the vampire's red lips, dripping blood. Gianni held it to Franklin's mouth.

"Please don't make me force you," he begged, emotion heavy in his eyes.

Franklin was dying. He could hardly keep his lids open or grip the vial hidden in his hand. Gianni held him up with his free arm, cradled against the vampire's chest. A part of him was appalled at the thought of drinking blood, but the part which wasn't ready to die overruled it. He wanted to live, and he wanted this vampire for his own.

Franklin opened his mouth, and Gianni pressed his wrist against it. He closed his lips over the wound and drank.

Instant euphoria hit him like a drug shot straight into his veins.

Gianni was murmuring to him, soft things like, "Good… there, there, drink, yes…" but he only half heard them.

Waves of energy filled every corner of his body, splashing through his system, and every caress brought with it more power. He shut his eyes against the onslaught. Taste overwhelmed his other senses: tart cherries and copper flooding his tongue, gushing down his throat and filling his belly.

Someone moaned. Maybe it was him. He couldn't tell.

It was over as quickly as it had begun. While Gianni tore his wrist free and licked it closed, Franklin ducked his head, spat a mouthful of blood into the vial, and capped it off, tucking it back into his pocket. He wanted more blood. He was desperate for it. He reached for Gianni's arm to bring it back to his mouth.

"No," Gianni ordered, yanking his arm away. "We have to leave. Snap out of it."

Franklin wailed. He wanted more of that power. More blood. More ambrosia.

Gianni slapped him. *Hard.* "Richard. Control yourself."

Ugh, Richard. That brought him to his senses. He still had to deal with that lie. Now that he felt such power, maybe it would be easier.

Gianni pushed Franklin off him and stood, extending his uninjured arm to help Franklin up.

Clambering back to his feet, Franklin felt strong. The pain at his neck and biceps was gone, and he thought he could run a marathon. Or pick up a car.

Or fuck a vampire.

Franklin discovered Gianni anew. That graceful, supple body. Lean muscles curving over his delicate frame. But not so delicate. Gianni had almost taken out Hutch. Would have, maybe, if the fight had continued. Franklin wanted to see what the vampire looked like under him, squirming with need. He reached for Gianni and took him by the back of his neck, dragging him in tight.

Gianni came but dodged the kiss. His lips were on Franklin's ear. "I'm flattered. Really. Now snap the fuck out of it—we have to get out of here." Gianni had hold of the sensitive skin at his waist and pinched it viciously. Franklin yelped and let go of Gianni's neck. The vampire backed away.

"You good? Can we go now?"

Right. They should leave. Vampires were coming. What the hell had he been thinking? "Yeah, sorry. Let's go."

Gianni held out his hand. Franklin took it and let himself be led when Gianni took off running. Even at this breakneck speed, keeping up was easy. That was some kind of blood in his system. The vial of it should keep the Scourge off his back and buy them more time.

Franklin didn't know where they were going, but he was glad they were together.

13

SAFE HAVEN

Gianni

They ran to the city lot where Gianni knew Richard kept his car. Staying in Bristol Springs tonight was not an option. They'd need to get out of town for a few days, at least until they got their stories straight. He had to let Hayleigh know he was okay before she told the council what *really* happened. Surely Richard would have to do the same. How the fuck were they going to explain?

When they arrived at the car, Richard stood staring at him. Gianni thought his eyes looked clear, but the lingering effects of his blood would still be in his system. The slayer must have felt high.

"Maybe I should drive." Gianni extended his hand for the keys, but Richard didn't hand them over.

"Where are we going?"

"I don't know. Anywhere. Somewhere to think. Out of town. A hotel?"

Richard nodded. "A hotel out of town. Got it. I'll drive." He opened the passenger side door for Gianni.

"You sure you're good to drive?"

"I feel great. Promise."

That was good. If Richard drove, he could text Hayleigh. The sooner the better. Gianni got in.

I'm safe. You okay? he sent, then sat back in his seat, glancing over to Richard.

The slayer seemed fine now. Gianni's blood had healed the wound on his neck and must have been thrumming through his veins. He was dealing with it well.

Gianni's phone chimed.

Hayleigh *I'm fine. Are you okay?*

Glad his friend was safe, Gianni replied, *Yes, fine too.*

Hayleigh *What the fuck, Gianni?*

Hayleigh *You owe me an explanation.*

Hayleigh *What am I supposed to say?*

Gianni turned the phone to silent. The hell if he knew. To get Hayleigh to safety and convince her to leave him alone with two slayers, he'd had to tell her he was safe with Richard. She didn't believe him, so he'd let her sway him right there in the middle of the street. He couldn't tell how much she'd gleaned from that little peek into his mind, but she knew enough.

He typed his response quickly. *Anything but the truth. Please. I'm in enough trouble lately. I can't have the council find out I'm dating a slayer.*

He stared at his phone and waited.

Hayleigh *You're lucky you saved my life. I'll come up with something.*

Thank you! Love you! I'll be back in a few nights, I swear. We'll sort it out. Gianni pushed send and relaxed a bit more in his seat.

Hayleigh *When you get back, you'd better tell me EVERYTHING. Promise.*

Gianni would tell her all of it. Getting it off his chest would feel good, and he knew Hayleigh cared. But what about

Richard? He would need a cover story too, and he didn't strike Gianni as the type who could pull off a lie. Gianni would have to think of an excuse for him.

"Gianni?" Richard interrupted his train of thought.

"Yeah?"

"Are we...bonded now?" Richard's voice carried a wobbly timbre, hesitant but still amped up on adrenaline. Of course he'd be worried about that, of all the things they had to be worried about.

Gianni sighed. "Not really, no."

"What's that supposed to mean?"

"Only a little." Gianni stared out the window. They'd left the city and merged onto the interstate. Trees lined this corridor of the county. There were towns along the way; they'd find a hotel soon enough. "We'd need to exchange a lot more blood to be bonded, and to strengthen the bond, we'd have to repeat the exchange often. Plus, I would have to drink from you, and I haven't."

"So what do you mean by *a little?*"

"My blood has addictive qualities. Not just for you, for both of us. You'll want to drink from me again, and I'll want to let you." He hesitated before adding the next bit. "It's also a natural aphrodisiac, but I already want to have sex with you, so nothing's really changed. At least for me." Gianni let the unasked question dangle between them, but Richard didn't rush to answer, so he continued. "The temptation won't be so great that we can't make our own decisions. Not after only once. You're not trapped, if that's what you're worried about."

"You're telling me the truth."

It wasn't a question, but Gianni answered anyway. "Yes. Rather kind of you to finally start believing me."

"You could have compelled me back there. I felt it in my spine. I wouldn't have been able to resist."

"I would never do that to you unless I had to. I only want *the real you*. I don't want an imposter."

Richard had nothing to say.

Gianni was in a contemplative mood and embraced the quiet. He'd come very close to losing Richard. He wouldn't let that happen again. How could such a man be convinced to leave the Scourge?

Pulling up to a Hampton Inn three towns from Bristol Springs, Gianni got out at the lobby and left Richard to park the car. He booked the room for two nights—so they'd have a safe place to spend the day—and requested extra blankets. By the time the clerk handed him an armful, plus two key cards, Richard had entered the lobby and was hanging back, waiting for him. Probably for the best. Gianni wasn't about to try and explain the blood on his shirt to the clerk.

"What's with those?" Richard indicated the blankets as they made their way to the room.

"They're to go over the curtains and block out the light."

Richard opened the door for them. "Oh, right. I'll help." He took a blanket and shook it open.

Gianni scanned the room. It had a boring, modern look: two double beds, sleek dark furniture, flatscreen TV, white walls with weird abstract paintings, and a bathroom off to the side. Dull but sufficient. He saw their reflections in the large mirror over the dresser: two ordinary-looking men, unfolding blankets in the cold unremarkable room. They could have been anybody. Business associates, travel buddies, lovers. *Husbands.*

"You okay?"

Gianni was torn from his thoughts. "Yeah, just thinking. You?"

"I'm okay." Franklin handed Gianni a corner of the blanket

and stood on the chair nearest the window. "What were you thinking about?"

Gianni dragged another chair over and tucked his side of the blanket up and over the frame, bunching it in the gap and letting the rest hang as a double barrier. "I'm wondering what you're going to tell your boss. What will that other slayer say?"

Richard followed his lead with the blankets, and together they blocked out all the gaps where light could get in. "I don't know. Maybe nothing. Hutch isn't about to brag about a vampire he didn't get to kill."

"But if you don't show up in the morning, will they come looking for you? I told Hayleigh I was okay. There's no one you need to tell?"

"I usually report to the chief." Richard shrugged.

"So call him." They were done with the blankets and stood facing each other.

"And say what? 'I'm at a hotel with a vampire. Don't worry. He's friendly?' No way."

"I was thinking more along the lines of a family emergency or something. Like, sorry, you were out of your mind, but you had to get to dear Aunt Edna before she fell into a coma and died. I don't know. What would they believe?"

"Not that," Richard laughed with a smile. "Look, it's fine. I'll come up with something when we get back. I don't want to think about the Scourge right now."

Richard's emerald eyes were sparkling, drinking him in with unchecked greed. Gianni would feel better if he was sure Richard's boss wasn't out searching for him. What if they spotted the car? But the look Richard was giving him was hard to ignore. Maybe they could put off the excuses for a while.

Richard stepped toward him and took his waist. His warm hands felt divine sliding up Gianni's ribcage. He wanted this, but he had to be certain Richard did too, without the draw of his blood.

"Are you sure?" He tried to keep the vulnerability from his voice, but the question came out rough.

Richard didn't falter. "I am. Are you?"

"God, yes." Gianni fell into his arms against his chest, tilting his head up to be kissed. Richard's lips on his sent a tingle through his body. He placed his hands on Richard's shoulders and squeezed, reveling in their strength. Here was a body he could appreciate. Toned and trim but powerful. Bigger than Gianni and unmistakably masculine. Hard in all the right places.

Richard kissed with the enthusiasm of a teenager and the technique of a lover who'd had the time to learn what he liked. The combination made Gianni's head spin. He lost himself, opening his mouth for Richard's tongue and sucking it against his own. He shivered at the thought that this was only the beginning. They had the privacy of the hotel, and Gianni had the slayer all to himself.

Gianni whimpered into Richard's mouth and released him for a breath. Their eyes locked. "Take me to bed."

"Gladly," Richard answered. In one motion, he scooped Gianni into his arms. He kissed him again and gently laid him on the mattress. "Let's get these out of the way." Bracing one hand on Gianni's calf, he pulled off the designer boot. Gianni watched, leaning back on his elbows as the other calf and boot got the same treatment. Richard looked even more sexy at Gianni's feet, stripping off each sock.

Gianni sat up and reached for Richard, pulling him in and opening his legs as the slayer's weight settled against his chest.

"You're so handsome." Gianni ran his hands along Richard's back, memorizing the feel of every curve. "I've wanted you since that first night."

"You licked me that night."

Gianni grinned. "Foreshadowing?"

Richard swiped his tongue along Gianni's cheek. "You're delicious."

Gianni hooked his legs over the back of Richard's powerful thighs and thrust his hips up, seeking friction. He found the answering hardness against his own as Richard moved with him. Their lips met. Gianni untucked Richard's shirt and slid his hands under the fabric, fingers seeking the smooth skin beneath. He ran them along either side of Richard's spine, sucking his lower lip into his mouth. Their pace quickened, a promising tease.

Gianni broke off the kiss with a delighted giggle. "You're too much. I could come like this, if you keep it up. Could you?"

"Yes," Richard breathed into the skin of his neck, mouthing wet kisses along his collarbone. His hips driving down into Gianni's never faltered, their rhythm perfection.

"That's hot." Gianni reached down to squeeze Richard's ass, to press them even tighter together. "I want more. Take my clothes off, Richard. Take yours off, too."

For a moment, Richard only pressed his face into Gianni's neck, hiding himself as their motion stilled. Gianni was about to ask what was wrong when Richard surged up over him, dislodging Gianni's legs as he sat back on his heels. He started with the pants, bunching the peach blouse up around his ribcage while undoing the button and zipper. Gianni lifted his hips to help Richard pull them down his thighs and off his legs.

Sitting up to help with the rest, Gianni pulled off his own shirt, then helped Richard with his. They worked together, clothes flying. There was so much beautiful skin, Gianni didn't know where to start, what to touch first. Richard was every bit as gorgeous underneath those clothes as he'd thought. Gianni let his hands trail over Richard's pecs, his lovely pink nipples, the ridges of his abdomen. He pushed Richard down onto his back. It was his turn to be on top.

Richard went gracefully, holding Gianni's hips in each hand as Gianni straddled his thighs.

"So this is what you've kept hidden under those dreadful

work clothes," Gianni teased, a finger running straight from Richard's sternum, over his belly button, and down the fine brown trail of hair leading to his swollen cock. "Gorgeous. I should have asked you to get naked for me sooner."

Richard smiled under him, squeezing Gianni's hips. "Nothing compared to you."

"Don't be humble." Gianni mapped circles around Richard's cockhead, smearing a bead of wetness from the tip to the frenulum before taking the shaft in hand. He watched Richard's face for clues as to how he liked it, and oh, Richard liked it. His mouth dropped open, green eyes drifting closed as a huff of breath escaped his lips. Gianni's grip was firm, working him smoothly, with enough pressure right under the glans to pull a sweet moan from his lover.

Gianni licked his free hand and switched his grip, adding a coating of saliva to Richard's cock and gliding his palm from base to head.

Richard's eyes flew open, and his hands went from Gianni's hips to his lower back. He growled, "Come here."

Gianni lowered himself to Richard's chest and opened his mouth for kisses.

"Are you trying to make me come embarrassingly fast?" Richard asked between nibbles on Gianni's lips.

"You're so sexy like this. I can't resist."

Richard pushed him up, making room, and slid his hand between them. "Let me touch you."

"You don't have to." Gianni was suddenly concerned. "I mean, you've never done this with another guy, have you?"

Richard actually laughed. "You're worried about that? Don't be. I'm not."

Gianni squirmed as Richard's warm hand encircled his erection and gave an experimental tug. A promising start. He felt the electric buzz down to his toes. As Richard explored him, he couldn't drag his eyes away. Seeing his own flushed pink glans appearing and disappearing in Richard's hand short-circuited his brain. Richard set a tight, fast pace. Gianni stopped thinking and let himself feel the body beneath him, hard under his thighs. The hand gripping him, hot around his shaft. Richard's other hand squeezed his thigh, grounding him.

Gianni rocked in Richard's lap, hips undulating with the demanding rhythm. He basked in Richard's gaze, stretching his body and preening under the attention. Gianni brought his own hand back to his mouth and watched Richard's pupils dilate as he licked it wet. He took Richard's cock and pressed it against his own, gripping them together.

His own sensitive flesh, squeezed to Richard's, brought a new level of enjoyment he felt to his core. Richard followed his lead. It'd be scorching with less friction, so he took Richard's hand and licked it as well.

Richard moaned as Gianni sucked each finger into his mouth one at a time. He coated Richard's hand with saliva, then returned it to their shafts. Together, they stroked.

Gianni let Richard set the pace, moving quickly with a tight grip. Gianni felt it to his core.

"So good," Richard said, eyes never leaving their hands.

Gianni leaned forward, propping himself up, and brought their faces closer. Not close enough to kiss, but enough for him to study each subtle change in Richard's expression as he approached the edge.

Witnessing this uptight, rigid man open up so beautifully beneath him was exhilarating. That he liked it hard and fast was no surprise. Richard gripped tight, and Gianni matched his strength. Not his usual preference, but tonight it was splendid.

Richard was nearly there. His eyes begin to flutter, then close, and his belly tensed, head tilted back. When he squeezed his lids shut, Gianni knew he was trying to hold back.

"Don't wait. Come for me. I want to see you." Gianni's voice was low and dripping honey, sugar sweet on Richard's cheek.

Richard came in a rush with a wild thrust almost unseating Gianni from his perch. Thick creamy spurts coated their hands and Richard's chest. Their rhythm slowed, Gianni following Richard's motions expertly, milking him for all of it.

Gianni wanted to lick the cum from his pecs, but that could wait. Now he enjoyed the view of Richard coming down from his high in slow increments. His breathing returned to his control, and his gorgeous green eyes opened to Gianni's lust-filled gaze.

"That was magnificent," Gianni gasped, and Richard flushed under the praise.

"Now you." Richard gave Gianni's cock a firm squeeze. "What do you want?"

"Let me come on you. I want to see mine mixed with yours."

"Yes." Richard smirked, looking drunk on the thought. "Me too. Tell me how you like it."

Gianni placed his hands on either side of Richard's head and sat back on his haunches, pinning Richard in with his body.

Richard's hand slid easily over him now, his cum slicking the way.

"Slower."

Richard slowed. "Like that?"

"Mmm, yes. And twist your wrist at the end. Oh, god. Keep doing that."

It wouldn't be long. He was so hot for it. Richard was underneath him, relaxed and pliant, his hand working him smoothly. Green eyes on hazel. Gianni would keep his eyes open. He wanted to watch Richard bring him off. He didn't want to miss a second of his reactions, documenting them all for future exploration. Oh, the things he wanted to do with his sexy, sweet man. Everything.

Gianni felt the bone-deep sensation begin to overtake him. He held on, riding the peak of the wave as long as he could before crashing over it, mindless in his pleasure.

"Fuck, yes. Please…" he breathed, body tense, coming over Richard's hand and onto his chest. "Fuck."

Their eyes never wavered, the passion in Richard's gaze adding to the intensity of his orgasm. Heedless of the mess between them, Gianni collapsed into Richard's arms and kissed his lips, licking into his mouth.

Richard returned the kiss, holding him in a strong embrace. For a moment, neither moved, their mouths pressed together, breathing in unison, cum mixing together between their chests. Then, slowly, Gianni let his head fall to the side, pressing his face to Richard's neck and taking a deep breath.

Everything was hot and sticky, and Gianni couldn't find a reason to care, not when this was perfect. Their bodies fit together like they were meant for each other, legs tangled over the bedspread. Gianni kissed his neck and shivered when Richard trailed his hands along his lower back and over his ass.

"Next time. Promise me."

"Hmm?" Richard asked.

Gianni pressed his ass firmly into Richard's hands and moaned until he got it.

"Oh. *Oh.*" Richard smiled. "Anything. Whatever you want. I promise."

Gianni grinned. "I've been told I'm insatiable. Don't make promises you may not be able to keep, Richard."

14

THE CHIP

Franklin

*R*ichard.

Hearing the fake name flow from Gianni's lips with such obvious pleasure made Franklin's stomach churn. He couldn't tell the vampire now; it would break his heart. Gianni *trusted* him, and Franklin didn't deserve it. The guilt ate at his insides like a vulture ripping pieces off a carcass.

For a glorious moment, Franklin had forgotten what an asshole he was. Instead, there had only been blissful floating in a magical world where he loved and was loved. He held Gianni, still trembling in his arms, and kissed his spicy flesh, and everything was right in the world—until it wasn't.

Richard.

In the morning. He vowed to tell Gianni the truth in the morning.

For the next few hours they would shower and sleep. They'd cuddle and enjoy each other. Then sometime, after Gianni woke up, Franklin would tell him everything and beg for forgiveness.

For now, he held his lover close and wished he wasn't such a goddamn douchebag. Gianni deserved better, and Franklin would be better for him. He would.

Gianni stirred in Franklin's arms, rising from his chest and dropping a quick kiss to his lips. "Shower with me?"

Franklin couldn't say no. They took turns washing each other under the hot water, lingering longer than was strictly necessary, eager to explore all this new naked flesh between them. Gianni's slender form was lightly muscled: hard beneath the lithe plains of his back, soft at the supple rise of his behind. When their skin began to prune, they climbed out and dried off. Franklin wiped the steam from the mirror to check the bite wound on his neck, but there was nothing to see, like the brawl had never happened.

"Gianni, is this normal? Does vampire blood really heal wounds this completely?"

Gianni ran his fingers over the perfectly healthy flesh of Franklin's throat. "Not exactly. My blood is different."

"Different how?"

"Just more powerful medicinally, and with less of it." Gianni stroked Franklin's neck where the bite would have been, then down over his shoulder to his bicep. He wrapped his fingers around the solid muscle and squeezed. "A normal vampire would have been able to save you, but at greater cost to himself, and there'd be a scar."

"What kind of vampire are you?"

"Oh, come on, you're bound to know. You tell me."

"You were born a vampire, weren't you? Your heart beats, you're warm… You're alive, right?"

"Winner, winner, chicken dinner! Also, I can eat. And I'm hungry."

Franklin wanted to know more, but if Gianni didn't want to talk about it, he wouldn't push. "Yeah, me too. I doubt there's room service at two a.m. Vending machine or twenty-four-hour grocery store?"

"Vending machine, I don't want to go anywhere that involves pants."

"I'm pretty sure pants are required even for the vending machine. I'll go. What do you want?"

"Chips, candy, whatever? You pick. Do you need money?"

"No, I've got it." Franklin found his pants discarded on the floor with the rest of their clothes and put them back on. Reaching into his pocket for his wallet, he felt the vial. *Gianni's blood.* At once he felt both guilty and *thirsty.* Gianni wasn't wrong, Franklin definitely felt compelled to drink from him again. Hopefully, that would fade. He ignored it, shoving the vial deeper into his pocket, and grabbed his wallet.

"Be right back." Franklin padded down the hall toward the lobby and bought half the vending machine. He wanted Gianni to have choices. The plastic bags crinkled as he balanced the tower of junk food in his arms.

Arms full, he tapped on the door with his knuckle, which Gianni opened, still stark naked. Franklin grinned, thinking of round two, but first, they should eat.

Later, settled on the second bed, empty junk food wrappers spread at their feet, Franklin and Gianni cuddled together against the headrest.

"What will you do during the day, while I'm stuck here?" Gianni asked.

"I sleep most of the day too, but at some point I'll get up and get us real food. Is there anything you'd like?"

"Whatever you're having is fine. We'll need toothbrushes." Gianni's expression grew sly, and he winked. "And proper lube. Please tell me you'll get that."

"That's the best idea you've had all night." Heat rushed to his cheeks, but he asked anyway. "Should I get condoms too?"

"If you want. It's up to you. I can't catch, carry, or transmit any human diseases."

"Really?"

Gianni nodded. "We're actually different species, you and I, despite the similarities."

Franklin hadn't known for sure. "Are there many of you?" There were loads of undead vampires—humans who were turned—but how many like Gianni?

"Not many. Breeding is strictly controlled in most populations to ensure survival. DNA contributions and semen samples are required before we can be turned. I've already done my part."

Franklin had no less than ten follow-up questions. He chose the most pressing. "Turned?"

"Into a regular vampire, the kind you're used to. I thought Oswald would do it, but he was lying. I guess I'm glad he didn't, or I'd never have met you." Gianni smiled and kissed him.

Franklin returned the kiss, but curiosity burned. "Why would you do that, though? Be turned? I mean, you're alive now. Why would you want to be dead?"

"Undead," Gianni corrected. "Because I'm fragile, like you. I can be killed in all the ordinary ways. All born vampires are turned eventually. Who wants to risk dying when you can live forever?"

"I don't want to live forever."

"Don't you? Have you ever given it any thought?"

He hadn't. Humans lived a normal lifespan; vampires lived forever. He'd never questioned it, so why would Gianni? Of course a vampire would want to live forever in the same way most humans would not.

"I guess not," Franklin finally answered. "It's unnatural."

"For you, maybe."

"So, are your parents turned?"

"I assume so."

"You don't know?"

"I don't know who they are. I'm a test tube baby, a product of the best genetic combination to ensure diversity in the line. Most of us are."

"Wait, your whole species? Was what, created in a lab?"

"Well, not originally, no. The science is fairly new. But many of the modern generation, including myself, yes." Gianni laughed. "You should see your face right now. It's doing this thing…" Gianni mimicked him, his mouth dropped open, eyes wide.

"Sorry. It sounds crazy. What happens if a couple falls in love and wants to have their own baby?"

"They can. It's not outlawed or anything, but their DNA, semen, and egg samples would still be used in our breeding program. It's not common because most want to be turned long before they'd desire children. That's probably why we got so close to extinction." Gianni shrugged like he was bored. "Enough about me. Tell me about you. How do you know so much about dogs if your dad never let you have one?"

Another subject change. Frustrating when he had so many questions, but it was only fair. "For a while, I thought my dad would cave if I could prove I was responsible enough to look after a dog. So I studied up. Volunteered at a shelter until he found out and put a stop to it." Franklin still felt the sting. He'd shown up to walk dogs only to be turned away. The staff had said his dad had been adamant.

"No offense, but your dad sounds like a dick."

"None taken. He is."

"How'd you turn out so sweet?" Gianni climbed into his lap, knees straddling Franklin's thighs, bare skin over his cargo pants.

Franklin struggled to maintain his train of thought. "You're the only one who thinks I'm sweet."

"Good." Gianni sighed the word into his mouth and kissed him. He tasted of the chocolate candies they'd been eating, sweet and delicious. Inching off Franklin's lap, he broke their kiss with a popping sound.

"Then be a dear and take off your pants."

Late morning found them in bed, tangled amongst the sheets, the length of Gianni's body pressed tightly to Franklin's side. The vampire had flung both an arm and a leg over him, and Franklin held him firmly around the shoulders. A peaceful warmth surrounded them in the dark room.

Franklin startled to high alert when the space was suddenly and inexplicably drenched in light. He pressed Gianni closer to his chest, gaze darting from one end of the suite to another even as his eyes adjusted to the bright overheads.

Confusion gave way to dread.

They were surrounded by hunters.

His GPS chip.

The Scourge must have tracked him there. The thought had occurred to him, but he'd dismissed it. He was on a mission, not obligated to return each morning. Why would they follow him? *Fuck.*

Hutch, General Labat, and her entire team swarmed the room. Gianni was waking. Franklin sat up and maneuvered him behind his own body, shielding him as much as he could from their view.

Last through the door strolled Chief Darrow himself, an angry look on his face as he surveyed the room.

"What the hell is this?" he bellowed, coming closer until he stood at the foot of the bed, staring down at Franklin with disdain.

Gianni had a death grip on his flanks. "Richard?"

Shit shit shit shit. What could he do? This was bad. This was so bad. He spread his arms wide, a futile effort to protect Gianni. Could he say anything to get them to leave?

He would have to hand Gianni over. Now. And willingly. To have any chance at all of being allowed access to him in the labs, of keeping his job, of attempting a rescue unsuspected, he must cooperate.

Franklin leaned into Gianni and whispered in his ear, "Trust me. I'll save you." Then he turned to his commander, even as Hutch was speaking.

"I fucking knew it, Franklin. You're screwing the blood sucker." Hutch's triumph sounded bitter to Franklin's ears.

Franklin ignored him. "Chief, I know what this looks like, but I have my reasons."

"Get out of the fucking bed, hand over the fucking vampire, put on some fucking pants, and explain yourself, Franklin, before I let them take you too." The chief gestured to the team.

"Franklin?" Gianni's voice shook. He'd dropped his hands from Franklin's sides. Tears formed in his devastated eyes.

Franklin couldn't do anything. "Yeah. Franklin. Gianni, don't struggle. I don't want you to get hurt."

Franklin threw the covers over Gianni as he got out of bed and reached for their clothes. It was humiliating, but he got dressed in front of them. The silence was eerie as he handed Gianni his things. He fingered the blood sample in his pocket. Gianni wouldn't understand. The vampire would hate him. But there was no other explanation. He produced the vial and held it out for Darrow.

"I did it for this. It's his blood. I thought the lab could begin testing on that sample while I continued to acquire information directly from the target. It didn't occur to me you'd doubt me, sir, or I'd have reported this location myself."

Franklin didn't dare look at Gianni's face. He couldn't bear it. The thought almost overcame him, but he held his ground and gave orders to the team as if they were there on his command and not Darrow's.

"The vampire is fragile. You cannot treat him as you would an ordinary vamp; you might kill him accidentally. I've told him not to struggle, but as you've blown my cover, I can't say as to whether he'll heed the instruction. Be careful subduing him."

Hutch wasn't buying it. "Bullshit! I saw you with him last night. He's got to you."

"Silence, Lieutenant," Darrow ordered, taking the vial from Franklin and clapping him on the shoulder. "Franklin has a fucking sample of his blood. How else was he going to get it? We blew his cover for nothing, thanks to you."

Inside, Franklin breathed a sigh of relief. It was working. Darrow believed him. But how would he ever explain to Gianni?

"How would you recommend we proceed?" asked General Labat.

Whether she spoke to Darrow or Franklin, Franklin didn't know, and he didn't care. He answered with authority. "A tranquilizer would be best." *And easiest on Gianni.*

She nodded and began to load the gun. Franklin flinched; that wasn't what he meant. The gun would be painful.

"Do you have a syringe?"

"Yes, but that's not standard procedure. It's an unnecessary risk."

"I'll do it." Franklin held out his hand. Labat pulled a syringe from her vest and handed it over. Franklin steeled himself and faced Gianni. What he saw broke his heart.

Gianni had tucked his knees to his chin and clung to the blanket wrapped tightly around his body. He hadn't bothered with clothes—frozen in place, cheeks wet with tears, eyes wide with fear. Franklin wished he could signal to him somehow. *I'm on your side. I'll fix this. I'm sorry.* But even if he could, the vampire would never believe him. The betrayal hung in the room like fog, infecting every breath, blurring his vision, dampening his senses.

He approached Gianni. "I know you're confused. I don't want you to be hurt. This is the simplest way."

The gaze Gianni cast on him was staggering. Hurt gave way to anger. "Is that your professional opinion, *Franklin?*"

His real name from Gianni's tongue burned like acid.

"Give me your arm."

Gianni flung the covers off and stood. A collective ripple of anticipatory movement came from the team, but Franklin raised his hand in a fist. "Hold."

If Gianni's nudity bothered him, he didn't show it. He stopped directly in front of Franklin and tilted his head, offering his throat instead. Franklin was ashamed as the thought of the vampire's blood made his mouth water.

"So this is how it is." Gianni's voice was cold as stone, hard eyes locking tight with Franklin's.

Franklin couldn't manage words. He only nodded.

"You'll have to catch me when I fall." Gianni closed his eyes.

Franklin pushed the needle into his neck and depressed the plunger. Gianni staggered, and Franklin caught him. When he was unconscious, Franklin ordered Hutch to get the dark bag. Without emotion, he wrangled Gianni's body into it and gathered the vampire's things.

"All right, it's done," said Darrow. "File out. Wilson, carry the body to the van. Franklin, you're with me."

As the team left the room and Hutch tossed Gianni's body none too carefully over his shoulder, Franklin quickly slipped Gianni's phone from his leggings into his own pocket.

"Good work, Franklin." Darrow slapped his shoulder once more. "That was the easiest capture of my career."

Franklin filed out, trying to keep his eyes off the bag.

What had he done?

15

TESTING

Gianni

The irritating scent of cleaning chemicals stung Gianni's nostrils as he woke. Lights bore brightly into his retinas. Terror hit him like a nightmare, but this was real.

The slayer had betrayed him. He was a prisoner.

Gianni glanced around, trying to get his bearings. He was in a cell, metal bars—silver, no doubt—surrounded him on three sides, the only solid wall at his back. Outside the cell were worktables laden with test tubes, microscopes, and a host of other machinery he had no hope of identifying. White, sterile, horrifying. He'd never felt more exposed. Silver manacles on his wrists and ankles produced a constant dull ache where they touched his skin.

Gianni tried to sit up but couldn't. Nausea and dizziness overwhelmed him, and he gave up. The tranquilizers must still have been in his system. There was no way to know how long he'd been out. At least he was alone, and a sheet was draped over him. That beneath it he remained naked wasn't ideal.

Was this how Spike felt? Abandoned by those she loved, alone in a cage at the animal shelter, her fate entirely out of her control? This was no way to exist.

Gianni closed his eyes, and the pain of betrayal overwhelmed him, coming on like a train and running him over again and again. Richard—no, *Franklin*—had been playing him the whole time. A sob welled up from deep within his soul, and Gianni let it out with a ragged breath. He'd trusted the slayer, loved him. Told him secrets. Questions came back to haunt him. *What kind of vampire are you? Are there many of you? You were created in a lab?* Not questions to get to know him—information to bring back to the Scourge. Gianni had answered all of them like a lovesick pup.

And his blood. The slayer had stolen a sample straight from his wrist. If he wasn't already chained to this goddamn cot, Gianni would kick himself for being so stupid.

He sure knew how to pick them. First Oswald and now Franklin. Bitterness threatened to choke him. Gianni would die for his poor choices in men.

The slayer had said to trust him, that he would save him. All bullshit to gain his cooperation. He wouldn't allow himself false hope. Trusting Franklin had gotten him where he was; it certainly wouldn't get him out. Gianni would wallow in his misery, endure whatever the Scourge put him through, and then he would die. The end.

Gianni wasn't one to give up, but then again, he didn't feel much like himself at the moment.

Time passed. How much was impossible to tell. Was it day or night? Gianni didn't know that either.

A woman entered the lab and strode across the room to his

cage. She looked like a scientist: glasses, white lab coat, brown hair pulled back into a tight updo.

"You're awake. Good. Get up."

Gianni stayed where he was. He'd grown cold, his body stiff to the point of numbness. He had no incentive to reawaken it.

The woman took a sharp breath and continued. "Maybe you don't understand. Allow me to explain. I'm Doctor Lojan. You may call me Doctor. I have means to force your cooperation if you resist, but they'll be painful. It'll go faster and easier for us both if you choose to comply. If not, I'll have to provide a sample. Now, get up."

Gianni feared pain. He didn't want it, but he also couldn't bring himself to move. It was better not to care. If he proved useless, they'd kill him sooner, so he lay there and waited.

The doctor pressed a button on the wall, and his entire body lit like wildfire. Instantly, the extreme burning sensation raged across his skin, accompanied by a sick sizzling sound and the smell of burnt hair. His muscles seized and his limbs locked, hands curled to fists.

It stopped as suddenly as it had begun, but Gianni could only lay twitching from the experience. The pain slowly receded. Blood bathed his throat from where he'd bitten his tongue.

"I'll give you a moment to recover. Then I'll need you to stand and approach the bars, or next time, the electrocution will be worse. The entire cage is wired. That was setting one. There are ten."

Stomach roiling, Gianni sat up. No way could he live through that again. If he'd had anything in his stomach, he'd have lost it. He looked down at his arms. The peach fuzz hair that had covered them was gone, and track marks lined each forearm. What had they done to him? Taken more blood? Drugged him again? Jesus, he looked like a junkie.

Gianni brought his hands to his head and felt for his hair. It was still there. How many more settings until it burnt as well?

He didn't plan to find out. Gianni stood on weak limbs and approached the bars.

"What do you want?"

Franklin

Gianni's cell buzzed in his pocket. Franklin hurried out of the compound to the privacy of his car. He had to get away before he could deal with the phone, somewhere he could think. The Scourge was full of interruptions: cadets congratulating him on his catch, other hunters slapping him on the back. Darrow had given him full credit. Apparently sleeping with the enemy was a heroic tactic where the end justified the means.

Franklin constantly felt like he would vomit, but outwardly he had to maintain a proud façade: a lieutenant whose unorthodox plan had paid off with the live catch of the century.

His life had become a waking nightmare.

God knew what they were doing to Gianni in the labs. His imagination created horrifying possibilities. Franklin couldn't risk putting in a request to see him so soon, or Darrow might suspect he'd grown attached. Franklin had gotten the blood sample that made his story convincing only by sheer luck. Things could easily have gone worse.

Damn Hutch and his meddling. The temptation to blame the other slayer was powerful, but Franklin knew he was the only one at fault. If he'd only warned Gianni sooner, none of this would have happened. He had to get the vampire out, no matter the cost. Gianni's lively spirit would wilt in captivity, and Franklin couldn't bear to let that happen.

He couldn't do it alone. The Scourge was too well guarded, the labs locked down, and the jail cells nearly impenetrable.

Desperate circumstances called for some unconventional assistance.

Franklin sat in his car in the lot at the baseball fields. From there, he could see their park bench. He stared at the phone in his hand. Gianni's phone. Twenty-two messages. Seven missed calls.

He pressed "return call" next to Hayleigh's name. She picked up almost immediately.

"You'd better have a damn good explanation for keeping me waiting like this, Gianni. The council is breathing down my neck. You can't just disappear with a goddamn slayer and expect me to cover!"

Whoa. "Um, Hayleigh?" Franklin managed.

"Who is this?" Caution in her voice now. Fear. "Where is Gianni?"

"They have him. I need your help."

"Is this Richard? What do you mean they have him?"

"Look, it's complicated, but my name's Franklin. I'm the man you saw with Gianni in the alley. I'm Gianni's…" *boyfriend, lover, enemy?* "…friend. The Scourge has him. It's my fault, but it was an accident, I swear. I'm going to get him out. I need your help."

"The Scourge has Gianni?" She was close to hysterical.

Franklin felt the same way. "Yeah, yeah, they do. Please, can we meet?"

"No way. I don't trust you."

"I understand, but I can't do this alone. I'm going to need help from vampires to have any chance at all. You're my only contact. Please. Can you put me in touch with your leader?"

"My leader? We're not aliens. I can get you in touch with the council if that's what you want. Though I may have a better idea to save Gianni. The council's process is slow. They'll have to convene. There'll be a vote. I'm sure they'd attempt a rescue, but it might be too late."

"I'm all ears."

"It's dangerous."

"I don't care."

"I know who'd drop everything and take the risk for Gianni."

"Who?"

During the following pause, Franklin had time to fully experience the nausea settled in the back of his throat, threatening to explode.

"Oswald."

Shit.

VISIT

Gianni

On the third night—at least he thought it was night—Gianni awoke in his cell, the hunger pangs spiked to alarming levels. He'd been given no food and no blood. Water was only provided when he was so weak from dehydration he physically had trouble complying with orders. Repeatedly, they'd collected samples; soon, he wouldn't have any blood left. At this rate, dying of electrocution over starvation might have been preferable.

When Dr. Lojan arrived, he was set to beg, but it wasn't necessary. Her assistant, Zeb, tall and wiry with short blonde hair, approached his cage with a tray of food. Gianni's empty stomach clenched in response. Dr. Lojan went straight for the dreaded button on the wall. Gianni stayed perfectly still.

"Zeb is going to unlock your gate and place the tray on the floor. Do not move, or I'll be forced to use our security feature. If you make me shock Zeb, you'll regret it," Lojan said.

Gianni obeyed. Zeb left the food for him, exited, and locked the cell. Only then did Lojan back away from the button.

"You may eat."

Gianni's entire body ached, but he managed to crawl from his bed to the food, holding the bedsheet around him as he went. Some sort of hot cereal—oatmeal maybe—two hard-boiled eggs and a banana. He didn't bother getting off the floor. He just picked up the spoon and dipped it into the porridge.

"Don't eat too fast," the doctor warned, "and don't eat it all at once. If your anatomy is anything like ours, your stomach will need time to adjust."

She was probably right, but Gianni didn't care. He was starving. He shoveled the goop into his mouth, warmth filling his belly. If he paid for it later in stomach cramps, so be it.

They were taking medical instruments from cabinets and drawers, preparing for something. Gianni would ignore them for as long as he could. Their presence brought pain, the hours between their visits a lonely reprieve.

What was Franklin doing? Was he being rewarded for fooling Gianni? How long had he been planning this? *From the beginning.* The truth of it struck deep. Devastating didn't begin to cover it.

Gianni wasn't stupid—he'd known Franklin worked for the Scourge. He had known their relationship probably wouldn't pan out in the long run, but he'd thought they'd been friends. More than that. The burning anger with himself for believing it came and went. Trading anger for hopelessness was easier.

The oatmeal was gone, and Gianni started on the eggs. Already, his stomach showed signs of protest, but the memory of hunger drove him. Would they wait another three nights to feed him again? He'd save the banana, just in case.

Whatever Lojan and Zeb were getting ready for, they were nearing completion. Zeb stared at Gianni with an eerily eager cast to his gaze, making the food in Gianni's stomach feel poisoned.

"Gianni," Lojan ordered. "Get up. Come here."

Gianni knew better than to protest or stall. He rose and stood at the bars. Would they take more blood? Surely he couldn't keep up the brutal pace they'd set for him. His legs were wobbly. If the bars hadn't been silver, he'd cling to them for support.

Lojan stood across from him, her posture rigid. "Give me your arm."

Carefully, Gianni extended his arm between the rungs for the needle. He'd become desensitized to the stinging pinch; it was ordinary now. When Lojan instead produced a scalpel, Gianni found himself still capable of an adrenaline spike. The urge to pull his arm back overwhelmed him, but the alternative was the evil button. Panic activated his fight-or-flight response, only Gianni could do neither. Fear must have shown in his eyes because Lojan spoke up.

"No need to worry. I'm only taking a few skin samples. You'll hardly feel it."

Nothing about that statement was reassuring. Lojan wasn't cruel, but she wasn't kind either, a stalwart scientist who likely considered him much the same as she would a lab rat. Ultimately, her job was easier with Gianni's cooperation. She would say or do what she needed to, within limits, to ensure his good behavior.

"Can you numb it first?" It was worth asking.

Gianni was met with her irritated sigh. "Don't be silly. It's a simple procedure. I'll be quick."

Still not reassuring. Gianni resigned himself to the pain and tried not to flinch as the scalpel came down on his arm.

After collecting their macabre bits of flesh, Lojan and Zeb left. Gianni lay on his cot, trembling in his bedsheet, eyeing the bandages around his forearm. He was tempted to rip them open and lick at the wounds. If only he could have some blood.

Oswald's blood would have been powerful enough to heal the slices on his arm and ease the ache in his belly. For a moment, he indulged in hopeless longing for his old boyfriend. Oswald might have been an asshole who betrayed him, but he was preferable to the asshole who'd betrayed him *and* sold him out to the Scourge.

Better the devil you knew.

Gianni was drifting off to a restless sleep when the lab door's opening chime broke the silence. Dread consumed his gut. Were they back already? What would they take now? Gianni didn't know if he could bear a second round. He couldn't look. Instead, he hid his face in his bedsheet. The back of his neck began to tingle.

"Gianni?" A familiar voice invaded the space.

You've got to be kidding.

If Gianni were honest with himself, he had been wondering whether the slayer would pay him a visit. Apparently not content with his victory, he must have come to see Gianni's suffering with his own eyes.

Without moving or uncovering his face, Gianni asked, "Did you come to gloat?"

"Of course not. I came to bring you some things."

No way would he admit to being curious. Gianni remained frozen.

"Please? I have clothes for you."

Clothes would be an improvement. "Just leave them."

"Gianni, please. Look at me."

He wanted to. In spite of everything, Gianni wanted to get up and go to him. He also wanted to murder him and had thought up a host of fantastic things to yell, but he resisted. The thought that Franklin might use the button on the wall struck terror into his heart. He flung the sheet away and sat up. Naked.

Let Franklin see what they'd done to him. He'd lost weight, and both arms were black and blue.

Franklin had caused this.

The slayer stood frozen at the bars, his face contorted with misery. What the fuck did Franklin have to be miserable about? He held a pile of clothes in his arms, but that wasn't what drew Gianni's eye. The man held a note to his chest. Gianni stepped forward to read it.

They can hear us.

Careful what you say.

I have a plan.

I'll get you out.

Gianni sneered. Like he was going to believe Franklin now. He didn't know what the man was up to, but he was done trusting people. He raised his eyes to meet Franklin's.

"Well. Hand them over."

Franklin passed the clothes through the bars, tore the note in half, and crammed it into his pocket.

Gianni fingered the soft sweatshirt before setting it on the bed to pull on the pants. "Are you going to watch?"

"Oh, sorry." Franklin turned his back to Gianni while he dressed.

The material was a grey, lightweight, ring-spun cotton. After the scratchy bedsheet, it felt like heaven on his skin. The socks were a luxury better than anything Gianni had previously known. He almost felt like a person again. Almost.

"Okay."

Franklin whirled back to face him. "Is there anything else you need?"

"A key would be nice."

Franklin nodded sadly.

Pathetic. "So you chose to kill me after all, *slayer.*" Gianni wrapped his arms around himself. "I didn't expect it to hurt this much."

Franklin looked physically wounded. This was too easy. Temporarily fulfilling the part of himself eager for vengeance felt like a salve. And there was the other part, the side pained to see his lover in turmoil. That half wanted to reach out and offer comfort. Fuck that half.

Ultimately, none of this mattered.

"Darrow gave me permission to ask if you had requests. I know this isn't ideal, but you don't have to be miserable."

"Don't I? Phew, for a minute there I was pretty sure I did. Thank god you're here to tell me otherwise."

Franklin looked at the floor.

"I want blood."

"I'll see what I can do."

"No. Your blood. I want it now," Gianni demanded.

Franklin's mouth hung open.

Gianni pushed while he was gaining ground. He held out his damaged arms. "Look what they've done to me. I can barely stand. I need it, Buffy." Gianni resorted to his pet name and pressed his luck, gazing up through his lashes. "Please?"

He'd won.

The slayer was already rolling up his sleeve and passing his wrist through the bars.

Gianni snatched his hand and held it palm up. He trailed his fingertips along the delicate flesh of Franklin's wrist, then brought it to his mouth and traced the same path with his tongue. Franklin's pulse raced beneath his skin, and Gianni couldn't delay any longer.

He was on Franklin in an instant, embedding his fangs in the soft flesh of the slayer's inner palm. Human blood wouldn't be as nourishing as vampire blood, but anything would help. Losing himself in it, he drank greedily. This was his slayer, who tasted of delicious honeyed pears and guilt, and Gianni would swallow him whole if he could.

Franklin wasn't protesting. Would he let Gianni take all of

it? Did he really trust Gianni to stop before it was too late? They barreled toward that precipice together, Gianni's mouth on Franklin's skin, both of their hearts beating rapidly.

When Gianni felt Franklin's free hand in his hair, cradling the back of his head, massaging circles on his scalp, he came crashing back to his senses. What was this? Affection? Fingertips curled his hair gently. He might hate Franklin now, but he didn't really want to kill him. He tore himself free.

As the blood warmed his chilled body, confusion dazed his senses. Gianni licked the punctures on Franklin's palm and leaned into the man's touch. He couldn't stop himself. It felt good, Franklin's hand in his hair.

Maybe if he asked Franklin to kill him, he would show mercy. Make it quick. It could all be over with.

Gianni stayed silent.

There was nothing more to say. He looked up into the emerald green eyes he'd grown to love, and heartbreak overtook anger. Gianni turned away; he didn't watch as Franklin left. He couldn't.

***

Franklin

"You let him drink from you?" Darrow questioned, rising from his desk. "The hell were you thinking?"

Franklin had known this was coming. He was prepared. His story only had to hold for another twenty-four hours, and then, for better or worse, this would all be over. He'd already cleaned out his room, destroyed his logs, and mentally let go of his life. Everything was about to change.

"I can reestablish our bond. I'm certain of it. The vampire is weak. He's cooperating, sure, but when you start drilling him about the Farthing, he'll shut down. You need me on the inside, now more than ever." It sounded even better when he said it out loud. Convincing.

"He could have bled you dry. It wasn't worth the risk."

Franklin shrugged. "But he didn't, and it was." It wasn't like Franklin to speak to a superior officer like this. He wouldn't win over Darrow without confidence, so he forced it into his tone. "He wants it, the relationship. Without me, he's completely alone. I gambled, and it paid off."

He hadn't known how Gianni would react. If he were being honest with himself, even in their dire situation, even angry and afraid, he knew Gianni would never hurt him. But when his jaws clamped down on Franklin's palm, a spiteful expression had taken over his features. There were worse ways to die than in a lover's embrace.

Darrow waved a hand in the air. "Fine, fine. You have open permission to visit the vampire so long as you don't get in Lojan's way. I hope you know what you're doing."

"Thank you, sir."

That had gone better than expected.

Visiting Gianni in his cell, seeing what they'd done to him… It changed what he thought of the Scourge. His whole life he'd been a loyal soldier. For what? So they could kidnap and torture innocents? No more. Franklin was through.

Next, the meeting he dreaded—Oswald.

Franklin had no clever plan to ensure his own survival when he'd outlived his usefulness to the sovereign. The vampire would need him in order to get in and to lead him through the maze of hallways to find Gianni. Beyond that, he wasn't sure what would happen.

Oswald could kill him or take him hostage. If it came to it, he'd sacrifice himself for Gianni. There wasn't time to organize a plan B for his own safety.

Freeing Gianni was paramount. Franklin had gotten them

into this situation, and he would get them out. What happened to him afterwards didn't matter.

***

Oswald brought an entourage worthy of a leader of nations. Over three dozen armed guards stood in formation around the sovereign. The vampire had chosen an empty commuter lot on the edge of town for their meeting place. It was isolated—dangerous for Franklin, but he didn't have a lot of choices. He straightened his shoulders and approached the menacing group warily.

Oswald had dark hair, like Gianni's, but longer. It hung stick-straight to his shoulders, lending his aristocratic features a severity at odds with his words.

"Welcome to the tea party. Hope you didn't want any—we're fresh out." Oswald puckered his lips and pouted.

Franklin thought he couldn't hate the man any more, but he was wrong. The vampire looked like a pimp in his dark purple suit and shiny black loafers coming to a sharp point at the end of his feet. All he was missing was a stupid hat.

Oswald came forward, managing to appear threatening despite the ridiculous outfit. Franklin gave no ground, still as a statue until they stood toe to toe. Oswald was taller and wider than Franklin. He used his bulk to intimidate, but Franklin had nothing to lose.

"Hayleigh tells me my Gianni is quite taken with you. You must imagine my surprise, as I've offered to take him back, forgive all his past shenanigans, and yet here he remains. With you." Oswald sneered. "And I have to wonder why." Oswald held both hands out, palms up, and shrugged. "Gianni is a pushover for some decent cock. How's yours?"

Before he could react, Oswald's hand was on him, squeezing his junk. Franklin slammed his elbow into Oswald's nose and stepped out of his grasp. The vampire laughed as blood dripped down his face. Two of the guards stepped forward, but the sovereign halted their progress with a raised finger.

"Feisty. My, my, no wonder my pet likes you. Do you hit him like that, too? He's sexy when he's bleeding."

It was all Franklin could do not to attack. Maybe this had been a mistake. "I didn't come here to trade barbs. We both want the same thing."

"Oh really, and what's that? To rescue the princess locked in the tower? That's what you need me for, isn't it?"

"Yes."

"Get on your knees and say please."

Franklin's initial reaction was *hell no*, but he tamped it down. He needed this vampire's cooperation, and he needed it now. Gianni was not faring well. Any longer in the Scourge's laboratory cell, and he might never bounce back.

Franklin fell to his knees.

17

OSWALD

Gianni

Gianni spent hours staring at the ceiling. There were no clocks in his prison. He missed a lot of simple things, like being able to check the time. He couldn't sense the difference between night and day anymore. The random schedule Lojan kept was disorienting.

The doctor was there now, moving from computer to microscope to desk. She never spoke to him while she worked; words were for demands phrased politely as requests. Gianni had questions he hadn't bothered asking, but one was boiling front and center in his mind, though he was afraid to say it. Not because he feared Lojan's reaction—the doctor was predictably professional, if somewhat cold—but because he feared the answer.

Wallowing in hopelessness wasn't doing him any favors. Gianni got up from the cot and stood at the bars. He began small.

"Excuse me, Dr. Lojan, would you tell me what you're

working on?" Most people liked to talk about themselves and their projects. Perhaps she would too.

Lojan glanced up from the tray she was studying, tilting her head as she took Gianni in. He remained placid, attempting to infuse innocent curiosity into his expression.

"I'm cataloguing your blood samples. They've been shown to induce a rapid healing rate in humans. If we can generate an excess synthetically, it would be the greatest thing to hit the market since penicillin."

The Vampire Council would not want this secret exposed. Gianni was torn. Saving people was noble, but not at the expense of being hunted by all of humanity. Not that he could do anything about it now.

"Is it working?"

Lojan took off her glasses and set them on the table. "No, it's not."

That didn't bode well for Gianni; they'd keep taking samples.

"Why do you want to know?" Lojan's gaze narrowed, her lips a tight line.

"When I forget to feel terrified, I'm bored and lonely. I thought maybe you'd talk to me."

"I see." She stood and approached the bars, her lips pressed tight together like she was solving a puzzle. "There's no need for you to suffer unnecessarily. I won't invite your interruptions, but if you batch your questions, I'll make time for them each day before we begin. In the meantime, I'll see to it you get some books. I take it that will suffice?"

He nodded. "Yes, thank you." It was more than Gianni had expected. Books would be brilliant. He braced himself to ask the question burning a hole in his brain. "One more, please, before you go."

She waited.

"What's going to happen to me?"

She waved it off. "Nothing. You'll be cared for—fed, sheltered, clothed—as long as you behave." Lojan said all this like it was a perfectly reasonable arrangement. "Are you afraid you're going to die?"

No, I'm worried I'm going to live.

Franklin

It was a colossal betrayal—another one—leading a team of vampires armed to the teeth directly into the Foundry. Franklin had an idea to mitigate the collateral damage, but he couldn't guarantee people wouldn't be hurt. He trusted Oswald about as far as he could throw him, and he had to put a plan into action to stop the sovereign from suddenly ordering everyone's death.

As they neared the complex, Franklin texted every contact in his phone stationed at this location.

This is Lieutenant Franklin Denhart. Get everyone out immediately. I have confirmation a large pack of vampires are on a mission to rescue the one in the lab. They won't hesitate to kill bystanders. Repeat: Get everyone out immediately.

Under the circumstances, it was the best he could manage. He sent the text early enough for people to take cover, but too late for a defense strategy to be enacted. Now he could only hope for the best.

They arrived in six black SUVs. With Franklin to punch in the key code, they were able to coast right into the underground lot closest to the lab. In and out.

As they exited the vehicles, alarm bells rang.

"Mm...somebody knows we're here." Oswald appeared rather unconcerned. With twelve personal guards spread around him and another dozen following behind, of course he felt safe. The man didn't even carry a gun; he left that to his lackeys.

"This way." Franklin indicated the stairwell and led the vampires through the underground labyrinth toward the lab.

The hallway was clear, a good sign his message had been taken seriously. Franklin tore through the compound, vampires hot on his heels.

Around the corner, a cadet scurried behind a door and slammed it shut. Another froze in terror.

"Get out. We're not after you—just go," Franklin yelled before the vampires could get trigger-happy. The cadet ran ahead, dashing down an open corridor. Good, they were headed the other way. Franklin pressed on. It was only a little farther. Any minute now an armed team would be sent to intercept. The faster they moved, the better.

Franklin stopped at the entrance to the lab. He punched in his code for security clearance and held still for the retina scan.

Nothing happened.

The outer door to the lab remained closed. He tried again. Nothing.

"Damn it. My code's not working." He had to hand it to the Scourge—deactivating his clearance had taken them only minutes. No matter. They'd come prepared.

Oswald was already motioning to another vampire with a flick of his fingers.

"Stand back," said Oswald's lackey. He held a small explosive, which he affixed next to the locking mechanism. Everyone backed up and faced away from the blast. It detonated with an ear-splitting bang.

The door swung open wildly, hanging sideways off its hinges. Franklin barged through.

The labs weren't empty as he'd hoped. Apparently, the crew there had thought the door would hold.

"Get out. We're just here for the vampire," Franklin yelled. Scientists and researchers scrambled for cover. No one there was prepared to fight. "This way." Franklin made for Gianni's cell, hoping the vampires would ignore the bystanders.

No such luck. Shots rang out as vampires fired at the scattering people.

"Stop it! We don't have time for this," Franklin ordered. "A defense team could be here any second, and then it will be a bloodbath. Hurry!"

They'd gone over this. Stupid bloodthirsty undead assholes. "We're nearly there."

Oswald walked calmly amid the chaos. Only an immortal being accustomed to power could possess that amount of insouciance toward their surroundings. Franklin wanted to kill him all the more.

They were almost there.

"He's this way. Come on," Franklin ordered, sprinting ahead.

The door to the lab holding Gianni was unlocked. Franklin pushed it open, relief welling in his chest when he spied the vampire standing in the center of the cage. He looked spooked, but very much alert and fit enough to run. He would have heard the blast and the gunshots. Had he thought Franklin was coming for him?

Gianni's eyes widened when he saw him. Franklin reached out for him, but two strong pairs of hands gripped his shoulders, restraining him.

"The fuck?" Franklin protested, struggling against them.

His arms were wrestled behind his back and fastened securely with zip ties as Oswald pushed past him toward Gianni.

"Hey!" Franklin thundered. "Let me go." He flailed and kicked to no avail. The plastic bit sharply into his wrists. More hands dragged him backward, out of the room.

Franklin strained for a last look at Gianni, but Gianni's eyes were fixed on Oswald.

Gianni

The blast had startled him awake, and the following gunfire sent chills down his spine. Franklin burst into the room. So the slayer's note had been true. He was rescuing Gianni. Hope swelled within his chest, expanding his ribcage. It was the first deep breath he'd taken since he'd gotten to this awful place. Was he really going to be freed?

Oswald.

Franklin was dragged away, and Oswald stood before him, reaching through the bars, heedless of the silver.

"Gianni, my love. What have they done to you?"

Gianni stared at him, too tongue-tied to answer, but he came to the bars and gave Oswald his hands.

"Don't worry, I'm here to rescue you. Lars!" he called, and one of his guards approached.

"You'll need to stand back," said one of Oswald's cronies. Gianni had never paid them much attention. While he'd been the sovereign's consort, he'd outranked them. Gianni let go of Oswald and fled to the back of his cage.

Oswald gestured to him. "We're going to blow the lock off your bars. Turn your back."

With one last glance around the room, Gianni did as he was told. Franklin was nowhere to be seen, but Gianni couldn't worry about him now. He would take his chances with Oswald.

His eardrums rebelled at the blast, ringing loudly even after it was over. Oswald was on him in a flash, wrapped around him like a long-lost lover. Gianni stiffened, but only for a second. The comfort was too tempting. He melted into the embrace and felt his eyes fill with tears.

"Not to worry, little love, I'm here now," Oswald crooned. "You're safe with me."

Even as the words filtered past the ringing, Gianni knew they were false. He couldn't bring himself to care. He wanted to be safe. Oswald was hands down preferable to this damn lab.

"Get me out of here," Gianni said.

Oswald wrapped a hand around his waist and swept him from the room, a bunch of vampire thugs surrounding them.

Wrapped in a blanket and tucked against Oswald's chest like a doll, Gianni glanced around the SUV with suspicion. They were still inside the Scourge's evil complex. He wouldn't rest easy until they'd cleared the city's borders.

Oswald pet his hair absently. The touch was a dichotomy between reassurance and nuisance. Gianni both preened for and rebelled against Oswald's possessiveness. For now, it was easier not to resist. Ignoring his mixed emotions, he sank into Oswald's body and watched out the windows for signs of trouble.

He didn't have to wait long. A team of slayers, maybe forty people deep, stormed the parking deck and began shooting at the cars. Gianni recognized only one: Hutch, front and center. Gianni ducked instinctively, but Oswald never flinched.

"Nothing to fear, pet, bulletproof glass and bullet-resistant tires. Mere cosmetic damage is all we'll suffer. There, there." Oswald stroked his back.

Gianni pressed his face into Oswald's familiar chest, closed his eyes, and willed the gunshots to stop. He breathed in the elaborate scent of the sovereign's fussy cologne: bergamot, thyme, vanilla. The car's engine revved, picking up speed, and the gunfire faded into the distance.

Gianni took a deep breath and straightened his back, putting a sliver of distance between them. A glance outside confirmed they'd gotten away home free. He should have been relieved but was too numb for feelings. He wasn't sure how an inquiry about Franklin would be received. He asked anyway.

"What happened to the slayer I saw before you came in?"

"Ah, the man who imprisoned you? I have him now. He'll suffer for what he put you through."

Gianni's stomach sank. He hated Franklin for the betrayal but found no comfort in the thought of him locked in Oswald's basement cell.

"Did he help you find me?"

"With some persuasion, yes. He broke rather easily. Weak-willed, that one."

It could have gone down that way, but Oswald treated lies and truths as tools to support whatever outcome he desired. Gianni couldn't trust it, and he couldn't rule it out. Had they tortured Franklin into aiding the rescue mission as Oswald would have him believe, or had Franklin been the architect all along? Recalling the determined expression Franklin wore as he barged in, the hope in the slayer's eyes, and the surprise at being restrained, Gianni doubted Oswald's words.

He let the subject drop. Pushing further would only give Oswald information to use against him.

Gianni let the car's engine lull him. He'd gone from one prison to another, but at least these restraints would be familiar.

18

BASEMENT

Franklin

*B*lindfolded and restrained, Franklin was manhandled from the vehicle and into a building. He was forced down several flights of stairs to what was surely an underground cell; the metal clink of doors closing told him that much. Unable to stop his fall as he was thrown to the floor, the jarring impact took the breath from his chest. A kick to the ribs left him gasping for air. He braced for more punishment, not knowing when or where the next blow would land. A boot struck his shin. A punch to the stomach. Another kick in the ribs. Even after his captors tore off the blindfold and left, he remained curled on his side.

Gianni was free.

He kept repeating the mantra to himself, to remember the objective had been accomplished. It didn't matter what happened to Franklin now. He deserved this. From the start of this plan, he'd known it was a possibility, as was his death, which could happen at any time.

If they kept him alive, he might get out. The Scourge would

come eventually. The GPS chip in his neck was a beacon they wouldn't ignore. But it wouldn't be a rescue mission, not for Franklin, not after what he'd done.

He could only hope Gianni would be out by then. Surely the vampire wouldn't stay with Oswald. He'd leave, start over somewhere fresh, forget all this. Move on. Forget Franklin.

Franklin rolled his shoulders, and pain flared through his restrained arms. He tested small movements in his legs. Not as bad. His torso, back, and ribs hurt. If the spike of pain each time he inhaled was any indication, there might be a broken rib or two. It could have been worse. Hell, he'd had worse in training.

He rolled to his knees, shuffled to the damp stone wall, and leaned against it. Definitely a basement, cold and dank. Too dark to make out much. A musty smell. No windows. Farther below ground than an ordinary basement. It took three flights of stairs to get here.

Franklin's hands were almost completely numb, the zip ties slowing circulation to a crawl. He could still feel his fingers. At least he was pretty sure he could. It was hard to tell through the loss of sensation.

There was a pocketknife in his pocket they hadn't found. Little good it would do him, unable to open it, but knowing it was there was still somewhat comforting. They'd taken both his and Gianni's phones, not that he'd get a signal this far below ground.

Sometime later, Franklin was dozing when the slamming of a door startled him alert. Boots pounded down a wooden staircase. As he was squinting to see who approached, the lightbulb blinked on, blinding him. He heard a key unlocking his cell and the gate opening. Just as his vision was returning, rough hands stood him up and gripped his forearm, and a blade sliced through the zip ties.

His arms swung free, dead at his sides. The pain would set in any moment as blood returned to the numb flesh. Franklin braced himself.

"Boss wants you presentable when he comes to speak with you." It was a vampire, young-looking, but that didn't mean anything. Male. Maybe six feet tall, shorter than Franklin but stocky, built strong. If it came to a fight, his bulk would make him slow.

"Freshen up. Eat something," he ordered.

A second vampire carted in a series of buckets, this one smaller, lithe, built for stealth. Franklin thought of the knife in his pocket, but this wasn't the time. If he could incapacitate the small one, he might be able to outrun the big one… Tempting, but no. He didn't know enough about their schedules or how many were housed in this facility. Besides, pins and needles were beginning their searing creep from shoulders to elbow. He couldn't trust his reflexes right now.

Bigs and Smalls left him alone, blessedly with the bulb still burning. The basement was lined with cells much like his own, but he was currently the only occupant. Franklin eyed the buckets. Two were half full with water, one mostly empty with a layer of sawdust covering the bottom. So these would be his sink, shower, and toilet. Better than nothing.

He reserved one bucket for drinking. With the other, he wet his hands and splashed his face. The third he used for its intended purpose, then pushed it away to the corner.

Oswald did not keep him waiting. The sovereign appeared at the top of the staircase and surveyed his quarry from a distance. "Well, well, well… Have you made yourself at home? Are you enjoying my hospitality?"

Franklin had nothing to say. He stared openly while Oswald descended the stairs and approached the bars. The vampire wore an elaborate house robe of crushed velvets in oranges and browns, belted around the middle and hanging to his ankles. Did he ever wear ordinary clothes?

"We have some things to discuss, you and I."

"Is Gianni all right?"

"The little one is asleep in my bed, where he should be, and that's all I'll say on the matter."

"Let him go."

Oswald laughed, his mouth a twisted grin. "*Let him go*, he says," the vampire mocked. "As if Gianni was my prisoner and not yours? Really, the arrogance. I should have you whipped. I might. Gianni is free to do as he pleases, and he's chosen my bed. In a moment, I'll leave you to dwell on that."

Gianni wouldn't really stay with Oswald, would he? Not after the way the asshole treated him. If Gianni stayed, he'd be in danger. Surely he'd leave. Franklin could convince him—if Gianni would speak with him.

"If he's free to do as he pleases, tell him I'd like to see him. Let him come visit me."

Oswald tsked. "That is precisely what we need to speak of. I realize it's only a matter of time before Gianni insists on seeing you. I won't have you interfering with our...reconciliation." The word came out slowly and over-enunciated. "Listen carefully. You were tortured into helping rescue Gianni. Say it."

Franklin only stared. So Oswald would have him lie to Gianni? Franklin had had enough of that in his lifetime. He wouldn't do it.

"I see. I thought you might need a little persuasion. Gianni may be free to do as he pleases now, but that can change on my whim. You make a problem for me? I'll make a bigger one for Gianni." Oswald gave a little shrug, as if this were no big deal and not someone's life he was ruining. He lifted a brow. "Say it."

Mouth dry, Franklin ground out the lie. "I was tortured until I agreed to help you rescue Gianni."

"I knew you'd see it my way. Do be sure to be convincing. Now, I'll leave you to your thoughts...of Gianni...in my bed."

Oswald turned with a flourish, his obnoxious robe swishing around his legs.

Franklin focused on his mantra.

Gianni was free.

———

Gianni

Gianni was trapped.

Nestled in a sea of soft Egyptian sheets and down comforters, curled against Oswald's side, head pillowed on his arm, Gianni wouldn't be moving anytime soon. How would he ever break free of Oswald's sphere of influence a second time?

This evening, Oswald was being indulgent. Gianni had always liked this mood. He'd take advantage of it as long as it lasted. Later, he'd let the panic set in. Oswald had dangerous moods, and Gianni never had learned how to predict the doting boyfriend or manipulative sadist.

Gianni couldn't stay, not indefinitely. Even if it was tempting at the moment, tucked next to the powerful vampire, knowing nothing could hurt him here except the vampire himself. But he couldn't leave either, not while Franklin was still trapped in the basement. He might have been furious with Franklin for the betrayal, but he couldn't leave the slayer to a slow, painful death at Oswald's fickle mercy.

It was complicated. Oswald did save him, after all. Did that mean he owed the man now? How much was his tab, and what would settle the balance? Would Oswald let him leave without a fight?

The sovereign stirred beneath him, turning to place a kiss on Gianni's forehead. "I can hear you thinking."

Gianni snuggled closer. Despite his trepidation around

Oswald, he couldn't resist the support his body offered. It was a guilty comfort, but he'd take what he could get. "Can't help it."

"You never could, though it gets you into trouble." Oswald's hand drifted down Gianni's naked spine. He'd ditched the prison clothes as soon as he was behind closed doors, and Oswald hadn't given him anything to wear. Gianni wouldn't ask. When it came to this man, nothing was free. He'd rather be naked than continue to accrue debt.

"I know it's over, but I can't stop thinking about it," Gianni lied. Better Oswald think he had PTSD than know his mind was on the prisoner in their basement. "It's like it's still happening. The electric shocks and the scalpel."

"Darling, I'll never let anyone hurt you again. I rescued you, didn't I? You're safe with me."

Safe with Oswald. Right. He knew better than to let the comment pass without acknowledgement. "Thank you."

Oswald flipped them easily, pushing Gianni to his back and climbing over him, pinning him in with his body. He lifted one of Gianni's injured arms and studied the damage.

"What has that slayer done to you, buttercup?"

"Franklin didn't do this," Gianni replied before it occurred to him he should have held his tongue.

"Franklin," Oswald said slowly, menacingly, "put you in a cage and left you to die. I blame him for every mark on your precious body, even if you're too stupid to realize it yourself."

"I just meant the doctor physically did it, is all. Took blood, injected me with god knows what, then took my skin." He shivered. He didn't want to be talking about this.

"Here, lover, let me…" Oswald bent to lick the sores on his arms. His blood would help even more, but Gianni wouldn't ask. He didn't want it. When he broke free, the withdrawal wouldn't be worth it.

Oswald moved from Gianni's arm to his neck. The licks became kisses, and Gianni could feel Oswald hardening against his thigh. He didn't want this either. Cuddling was one thing, sex was another, and he wasn't interested.

"No." Gianni pushed against the larger man's chest. "Oswald, please."

"Please, what?"

"Please get off me. I'm not ready for this." The vampire stilled over him, fangs dangerously close to his carotid. It could go either way, and Gianni was at a loss as to how to tip the scales in his favor. "Please," he whispered, sounding pathetic even to himself.

Oswald rolled off him. "Have it your way." The vampire threw on his robe and headed for the door, probably to find someone else to fuck. "You need blood. I'll send someone in."

"Thank you."

It wouldn't be that easy next time.

19

REGRETS

Franklin

Three miserable nights passed before Gianni came to see him. Franklin doubted the vampire would come at all, but each time he heard the door creak open, he couldn't banish the hope it would be him.

Then, finally, it was.

There he stood at the top of the stairs, aloof and beautiful.

"Gianni," Franklin said without thinking. The name flowed from his lips like a prayer.

"Buffy," Gianni replied, eyes narrowed. "Or would you prefer Richard?" He descended the stairs but kept back, away from the bars.

"It's Franklin. I'm sorry about that."

"Oh, you're sorry?" Gianni's eyebrows lifted. "I guess that makes everything rosy between us. Shall we kiss and make up?"

Franklin stared at the floor. Gianni's cold expression hurt too much.

"I guess not, then. Franklin must not be much of a kisser. Funny, I remember Richard was thorough in that pursuit."

Franklin bit back the pain of Gianni's icy needling, trying to focus on what he meant to accomplish—convincing Gianni to leave. Oswald was bad for him, and at some point, when the Scourge was good and ready, they'd attack this location. It could happen in days or in weeks, no way to know.

Franklin remembered what Oswald had ordered him to say, but surely he wasn't meant to volunteer that information. Maybe Gianni wouldn't ask, and he'd be let off the hook.

"Hmm, yes," Gianni continued, "I thought you were quite electric in that department—kissing, that is—until I was actually electrocuted. It turns out kissing and electricity have nothing in common. Lucky for you these charming accommodations aren't equipped with such a feature."

Franklin winced. He deserved the lashing, but it didn't make it any easier. This wasn't like Gianni. "You sound like him."

Gianni froze, mouth open. Fury and disbelief coalesced in his gaze. "Is that your piss I smell? How embarrassing for you." Gianni wrapped his arms around himself, chin high, eyes half-lidded. "Tell me, how does it feel now that the tables have turned?"

Franklin saw through it all. The vampire was miserable, and he was hurting. This was Franklin's fault; he had to make it right. "I deserve this for what I did to you. I'll be sorry until the day I die. I never meant for any of this to happen—"

"Oh, shut up. Of course you did. It was your plan from the beginning. It's on me for being stupid enough to fall for it, but if you think I'll believe your lies a second time, you're mistaken, *Franklin*." He spit the name with venom.

"Gianni, no, I swear." Franklin came right up to the bars and grabbed them so hard his knuckles went white. "I was going to tell you everything. I thought we had more time."

"Then how the fuck did a dozen or so of your best mates come storming into our hotel room, huh? Better yet, explain the vial of my fucking blood in your pocket. Please. I'll wait."

Franklin was terrible with words. He longed to tell Gianni the whole story, but put on the spot like this, all he could do was stutter. "I…I was buying us time."

"Oh right, that. You wanted to fuck me before handing me over, is that it? Now I understand. What's a vial of blood between fuck buddies, eh?"

"That's not what I meant. It's coming out all wrong. I just thought—"

"Never mind." Gianni laughed, but he looked pained. The combination haunted Franklin. "I came down here to see if you were okay. I've realized I don't care." He turned to go.

"Gianni, wait, please. It's important."

The vampire stopped with his back to Franklin. "Well? I'm waiting."

"Look, you have to get out of here. It's not safe."

The strained laughter was back. Gianni spun round and strode to the bars, inches separating them. "Let me get this straight. You—who had me imprisoned, electrocuted, starved, and bled dry—now want me to believe you're concerned for my safety?"

"Yes. Desperately so. Because it's true."

Gianni tilted his head, his hazel eyes angry but also curious. "What do you think you know?"

"I can't say, but you have to get out. Gianni, I know you won't believe me, but I love you. I never should have lied to you. I'm not lying now."

Silence. Gianni stepped back once. Twice. The vampire stared daggers at him, the ferocity practically tangible. His breath came fast.

Franklin had gotten to him.

Gianni softened an iota. "Franklin," he said slowly, and without the sneer that had accompanied him to the cell. The familiar, curious expression Franklin had come to associate with Gianni was back. "Did you organize my rescue?"

Shit. Why did he have to ask? And now? Franklin had to give Gianni the sovereign's answer, or Oswald would trap Gianni here—or worse. If Gianni had any chance at escaping the man's clutches, Franklin would have to lie. Through clenched teeth, he forced out the words.

"They tortured me until I agreed to help you."

"I see," said Gianni as he left.

Gianni

He had to get away. Out of Oswald's house, off his property, and far from his influence so he could think. Gianni grabbed a set of keys off the mantle and stormed outside. He pushed the unlock button to see which SUV would be his ticket out for the night, then made a beeline for the flashing headlights, started the engine, and got the hell out of dodge.

Damn Franklin.

The slayer knew something he wasn't telling him. Again. And on top of it, he was definitely lying.

Of course Oswald had something to do with the lying. Who knew what the asshole had threatened. Gianni suspected Franklin was the engineer behind his escape, with Oswald swooping in to take the credit. Franklin's bullshit admission of torture confirmed it. It was exactly like Oswald to manipulate the situation to meet his own ends. Trying to make sense of it all, Gianni drove toward the suburbs and out of the city.

Fuck. That had gone so wrong. Gianni'd had no intention of saying half the shit that came out of his mouth, most of which he'd regretted before leaving the basement. He'd been worried about Franklin and had strategically waited several days to see him so Oswald wouldn't think it was important. Really, he wanted to scout the situation so he could begin planning a way to get them both out, but that wasn't what happened.

Seeing Franklin brought with it the devastation of betrayal. Anger loosened his tongue, and nasty vitriol spilled from his mouth without his heart's permission. Franklin made it so easy. Standing there dejected, taking everything Gianni threw at him like punches to the gut.

The things he'd said. Hateful things. Even if Gianni wanted to, he couldn't hate Franklin. He cared too much. Franklin had been kind to him, protective up until he wasn't, but if he was telling the truth, he hadn't meant for Gianni to be hurt. And it didn't help that the slayer was maddeningly handsome, despite the poor conditions of his captivity. A beard had begun to cover his cheeks. Gianni itched to touch it.

Franklin looked him in the eyes and said he loved him. What was Gianni supposed to do with that? It had been the truth, though it barely made sense.

Gianni needed a phone and an internet connection immediately. The only place he could think of at this time of night was a twenty-four-hour Walmart. He punched it into the SUV's GPS. Oswald could track him, but he'd have to take the risk. He'd buy other things as well, frivolous trinkets to cover the shopping trip, and hope this was over and done with before the credit card bill exposed his sins.

Maybe Oswald wouldn't notice.

Gianni tore through his bags in the brightly lit parking lot. He needed access to his own money and to move it to a safe location. He'd need new bank accounts that couldn't be traced. When this was over, he and Franklin would have to disappear. Gianni would arrange to buy a car and supplies.

If he was lucky, it would only take a week. He didn't want to think how long it might take if he wasn't lucky. How long until whatever Franklin was worried about happened?

The more Gianni thought about it, the bigger the mystery became. Why would Franklin want Gianni to get out? Well, he wouldn't want Oswald to fuck him. But there was more to it. Franklin wasn't a jealous boyfriend. Gianni believed he cared for his safety.

Did the slayer think the Scourge would come for him, even after what Franklin had done?

If Gianni was right and Franklin had been the one to stage his rescue, it meant he'd betrayed them. They wouldn't risk men to save a traitor. Even if they would, how would they know where Franklin was? Oswald was nothing if not paranoid about his privacy.

Gianni followed the GPS's instructions back to Oswald's house.

The GPS's instructions…

The GPS!

Was Franklin wearing a GPS chip? He was still in his own clothing. Surely bugging was a possibility. Could the Scourge track him?

That would explain the men in their hotel room.

If Franklin was a traitor, the Scourge wouldn't be coming to rescue him. They'd be coming to kill Oswald and any vampire left standing. That's why Franklin wanted him gone.

Gianni cursed himself for waiting three nights. He'd wasted time and had no way to know how much they had left.

Fuck.

Back in the house, Oswald noticed his return and greeted him at the door, arms reaching for his bags. Gianni had pocketed the phone and thrown out the packaging. All that was left were scarves, purses, shoes, and snacks, things Oswald would expect him to buy anyway. He let the man take his bags.

"Did you have a nice shopping spree, pet?" Oswald set the bags on the hearth and took Gianni by the waist.

"Mmhmm, yes. I needed that." Gianni kissed him because Oswald expected him to. "Thank you," he mumbled against his lips and pulled away. "I got you something."

"Oh, really. And what, pray tell, did you buy me with my own money?"

"Since when have you been stingy with money?" Gianni sorted the bags until he found what he was looking for. He hadn't bought it for Oswald; he was improvising.

"I'm only teasing. You might have told me you were leaving —I'd have come with you."

"I needed some time alone." Gianni laced the emerald and gold scarf around Oswald's neck. The green had reminded him of Franklin's eyes. "You've never begrudged me that before."

"And I wouldn't now." Oswald took Gianni's hands in his. "Thank you for the scarf. It's delightfully quaint." The vampire kissed his fingers. "You went to see the slayer. What did he say to you?"

Of course Oswald would ask.

"Not much. Mostly I yelled at him until he confessed to helping rescue me only because you made him do it. Nothing I didn't suspect. Let him rot down there." Gianni draped his arms around Oswald's shoulders and pressed their chests together. Couldn't have the man thinking too hard on Gianni's whereabouts. He would need a lot of leniency in the coming nights if his plan was to have any chance at success.

If Oswald needed some reassurance of Gianni's loyalty, Gianni would have to convince him.

PACKING

Franklin

Gianni's words gnawed at his mind. Franklin replayed every nasty thing the vampire had said. He'd known Gianni would hate him for what he'd done, but hearing such venom slip smoothly from his lips had been harder to take than he'd imagined.

He deserved all of it and more. The realization of just how wrong he'd been about vampires hit him with a gut-churning wallop. The Scourge reduced vampires to parasites—mindless predators feeding off and killing innocent people for pleasure. It had been drilled into Franklin since childhood.

But Gianni wasn't a monster. The vampire was kindhearted, vulnerable, and witty. He could love the same as any man. If Gianni was different, what did that mean about the others? Hayleigh was a caring individual. Her concern for Gianni moved her to provide instrumental help in his rescue.

How many innocent vampires had he slain?

How much of his life was a lie?

Then there was Oswald. That lying sack of shit was what the

Scourge existed to exterminate. He needed slaying, and Franklin was the hunter that would do it. He'd rid Gianni of Oswald's bullshit forever.

Not that he could do anything from this cell.

The door creaked. Even though Franklin desperately hoped Gianni had heeded his warning, part of him still wanted to see the vampire at the top of the stairs.

No such luck. Speak of the devil, and he shall appear.

Oswald descended the steps.

Franklin couldn't stand the sight of him; he watched a bug on the wall instead.

"And how are we this fine evening?" Oswald said.

Franklin didn't bother with an answer.

"Come now, don't be rude. I came to deliver a reward."

What the hell did he mean? "A reward for what?"

"Being a good little boy and confirming for Gianni who his hero really is." Oswald spread his arms, palms up, as if speaking to a crowd and not a single, uncaring prisoner. "You must have been very convincing. My little bed-warmer's been quite needy since visiting you."

Damn it. Gianni hadn't left yet. This was shit news. Then again, he couldn't trust anything Oswald said; Gianni wouldn't really go back to sleeping with him. Gianni might have hated Franklin, but he also hated Oswald.

"Bullshit. You're not sleeping with him. Gianni's moved on."

"I wouldn't want to believe it either if I were you. After all, you thought you were going steady, didn't you? Gianni goes all sweet for you, lets you fuck him a bit, and suddenly you think he's yours. But Gianni's a wildcat in the sack. He needs more than one cock to fill him up. In fact, you should see him take three at once. It's really a sight." Oswald chuckled. "Maybe I'll let you watch."

"I don't believe you," Franklin barked, disgusted.

"Suit yourself." Oswald gave a half shrug and came a step

closer to the bars. "I shouldn't let you have your reward after such behavior, but I know you miss him. And I can be generous." The sovereign threw something into his cell. "Those should hold you over for a bit. He really filled them out nicely, just bursting at the seams. You can picture it during your free time."

Oswald's laughter filled the basement as he left.

Black lacy panties lay on the floor of his cell. Fresh semen stained the front.

No way. Gianni was better than that. Maybe he was gone after all, safe and sound in some new town, forgetting about all of them. Oswald was taking out his frustration on Franklin, but Franklin wouldn't let the man get to him.

The sovereign would be dead soon enough.

Gianni

His phone chimed on the dresser across the room, but Gianni was in bed high as a fucking kite. For all the effort retrieving it would take, it might as well have been at the bottom of the ocean.

Oswald had offered his blood, and refusing might have blown Gianni's cover, so he drank. He drank so much he could feel colors. Blue felt especially nice, like waves rocking him back to sleep. He closed his eyes.

The phone chimed again.

It might be important. In fact, Gianni was sure it was important, seeing as only one person had his new number, and that was Tabea. He'd found her again through the donor directory and enlisted her help in getting back in touch with Hayleigh. He'd ghosted on both women and owed them explanations. Plus, he would need their help.

Gianni rolled over to his stomach and pressed up onto his hands and knees. It seemed safer than trying to sit up directly, but doing so made him dizzy. Oswald was old, nearly two centuries, and his sire had been ancient. The combination made his blood the strongest Gianni had ever sampled, usually sipped in small doses either for bonding, healing, or as an aphrodisiac. In their shared history, it was often used for all three at once. Oswald liked it rough, and Gianni regularly needed his blood's medicinal properties in the aftermath.

Tonight, Oswald had given him a river, and his body could hardly contain it. He felt the current in his bones. This much blood would re-addict him—surely Oswald intended to have Gianni dependent on him once more. The plan worked. Gianni would now need regular infusions to function. A damnable step backward, but sometimes one had to go back to move forward.

The blood bond threw a wrench in Gianni's plans, but he'd detoxed from the powerful elixir twice now. He could do it again. Gianni sat back on his heels and knee-walked to the edge of the bed. He could see the phone from there, but could he stand up? The thought of Oswald seeing incriminating messages before he could delete them motivated him to try.

Slowly and steadily, Gianni put his weight on his feet and managed one foot in front of the other until he could collect the phone from the dresser and fall back into bed. Success. He wedged himself against the headboard and looked at the screen. Tabea must have been successful because the messages were from Hayleigh.

Unknown *Gianni? Tabea Perez gave me your number.*

I've been so worried about you! No one would tell me what happened.

Are you okay?

Gianni programmed the number into his phone and replied, sobering up enough to type.

Gianni *I'm sorry I scared you. Am okay now. Back in Philly.*

Hayleigh *Are you with Oswald? Are you sure you're okay?*

Hayleigh *Can I help?*

Gianni *Yeah. I'm sure. Can you tell me what happened? Did Franklin contact you, because nothing else makes sense.*

Hayleigh *He did. He said the Scourge had you, and he wanted to talk to our leaders to stage a rescue. I thought Oswald would be faster. Was I wrong?*

The final confirmation fell into place. Not only had Franklin saved him, the man had sacrificed himself to do it.

Gianni had to get him out of there.

Gianni *No, you weren't wrong. You were great. I want to tell you everything, but I have to delete all these messages. We'll have to start over and be more careful.*

Gianni *Can't trust Oswald not to check my phone.*

Hayleigh *Just tell me what to do.*

Gianni *Can you help me pack my stuff? He'll let me visit if it's to get my things. I can fill you in then.*

Hayleigh *Of course.*

Gianni *Okay, let's start over... Text me back, send the first messages again. We'll go from there.*

Gianni deleted the texts, and they had the conversation again. He would ask to borrow a car to get his things. Better yet, he'd ask for a driver. Then Oswald would have no reason to be suspicious of his motives. When the sovereign inevitably read the texts, they'd only back up the request.

As he lay flat on the sheets, the high which had begun to wear off during the serious conversation came slamming back. Gianni closed his eyes and saw green behind his lids. Green felt like Franklin. The tingle in his spine was absent, but the slayer's eyes sparkled in his imagination. Dream Franklin kissed him. Gianni moved his hand to his cock, stroked himself, and pretended it was his slayer.

Being at the Farthing again brought no comfort. The vampires there hadn't liked him before he'd gotten himself captured by the Scourge, and they definitely didn't now. It was a long trip; they'd have to stay over a day. Gianni had arranged to stay with Hayleigh so that his driver, Bart, could take his room. He and Hayleigh were assured plenty of time alone.

They'd packed everything that would fit in the SUV. All there was left to do was sleep and head back to Philly. He settled next to Hayleigh in her bed, tired to the bone. Planning a jail-break and consequent escape was exhausting.

Hayleigh was propped on her side, wearing pale yellow pajamas with suns on them, waiting for the full story.

"I thought Bart would never leave. Tell me everything—you promised," she said.

"I will, I swear, from the day I met the slayer until now." Gianni grinned. "But first we have to discuss what you're wearing."

She looked at her chest, covered in rays of sunshine. "What's wrong with what I'm wearing?"

"You're a motherfucking vampire! What's with the suns?"

She laughed. "They're cheery, okay? I like them. Plus, you can't tell me you don't appreciate the irony."

He joined her in laughter. "Oh, I do." Feeling normal again was amazing, if only for one day. By tomorrow night when they woke, he'd be jonesing for Oswald's blood, and reality would smack him back down. But for now, he had a confidant and a story to tell.

He began with the night he confronted his stalker and ended with, "I just have to break him out of Oswald's basement before the Scourge comes to kill us and then find somewhere to hide, possibly until we die."

Hayleigh was silent. Gianni added, "Don't worry, I have a plan."

"Oh, as long as you have a plan," she began, rolling her eyes. Then softer, "You've got it bad for this guy."

Gianni sighed. "Apparently."

"You're crazy, falling for a vampire slayer. And don't talk about dying—someone will be honored to turn you."

"I can't even think about that right now. I'm too worried about what the next week will bring."

"How are you going to get out? Is there anything I can do to help?"

"Well, the plan involves some offshore bank accounts and temporarily living in a van, but I think I have that covered. There is one thing you could do…"

PERIL

Franklin

There was a lot of time to think when locked in a cage alone in a vampire's basement. Days and nights ran together. According to Franklin's tally of hash marks in the dirt on the floor, he'd been there nearly two weeks. He was fed, but not enough, and his water and toilet buckets were changed daily. He'd been given a towel and soap but nothing new to wear. Putting dirty clothes over a clean body was its own kind of torture. Otherwise, he'd been left alone to rot.

Franklin was growing thin from the reduced diet. He'd halved his exercise regime to compensate for the lack of calories. The longer he waited, the more unlikely an escape attempt would be successful. There were at least six different guards, maybe more, and they always came in pairs. He'd have to incapacitate and outrun two immortal beings with only a pocket knife as a weapon, and it wasn't even silver. That was only to leave the basement. He didn't know what lay waiting in the stories above.

His father would have learned what he'd done by now.

Cameras in the main hall would have caught it all. Denhart Senior would assume Franklin was dead, and he was probably glad, after the shame Franklin had brought him. Franklin tried to feel sad and found he couldn't. His father had never cared enough to get to know the real Franklin, only the soldier. Only the hunter mattered to him. What harm could letting Franklin have a dog have done? He thought of Spike and hoped she'd found a good home.

It was endless, the thought spiral and the guilt. Franklin wallowed in it, absently stroking the beard he still wasn't used to having.

Gianni had not come back to see him. With all his heart, Franklin hoped the vampire had heeded his warning and left.

It was only a matter of time before Oswald killed Franklin or the Scourge killed Oswald. They'd plan their attack for dusk, when any daytime security systems the sovereign might have in place went offline. The vampires would just be waking and could be taken by surprise. Franklin listened for disturbances upstairs, but all was quiet.

Would the Scourge kill Franklin when they discovered he was still alive?

Or would he simply be trading prisons?

Gianni

All the elements of his plan were ready, but that did nothing to assuage Gianni's terror. This was going to be risky, and even the best-case scenario still came with a week's worth of painful withdrawal symptoms. It was early evening, the brief window he could go outside in the twilight when other vampires had to stay indoors. Oswald had no human staff, which meant if he could get Franklin out without waking anyone, they would have a short head start.

Oswald slept soundly beside him. Already, Gianni wanted his blood; his veins ached for it. The sovereign had been thorough in his entrapment, giving him copious amounts of blood more often than ever before. Recovery would be a struggle this time.

Gianni slipped from the bed and padded over to the bathroom. He only needed to take four things with him: a key to the basement cell; keys to the van; his phone; and Franklin. Everything else was stashed two blocks away in the cargo van he'd purchased.

Some elements of the plan had been easy, like acquiring keys to Franklin's cell. He'd done such a good job of convincing everyone he didn't care about the slayer the keys were hardly guarded. He'd nicked one, made a copy, and had it back on the guard's belt without anyone being the wiser.

Buying a commercial vehicle had been more challenging. The money took days to transfer to his new account. After persuading a salesman to stay late, then came excuses to leave the house early. Finding a van with no windows and an empty cargo hold took several nights. The purchase itself took time, as the paperwork had to be submitted by the finance officer during the day. Gianni had driven away triumphantly in a high-top sprinter van the size of a small house.

More time ticked by as he supplied the van with everything they'd need for the week it would take Gianni to cycle through the withdrawals. He'd no idea what condition Franklin would be in, so he'd stocked first aid supplies. Everything was safely locked away in the cavernous vehicle.

All that was left was collecting Franklin.

Gianni tiptoed from the bathroom, through the hall past the guards' rooms, and down the stairs to the lowest level. Carefully, he opened the door to avoid the creaking sound, and there was Franklin, doing pushups in his cell. Gianni made it halfway down the stairs before Franklin noticed him. The slayer sat back on his haunches, eyeing him from behind the bars. If Gianni had to guess, he would say the man looked disappointed.

"Gianni," Franklin said. "What are you still doing here? It's not safe."

Oh well, Gianni couldn't expect a warm welcome after the way he'd treated Franklin last time, though the slayer's worry was sweet. "Shush, keep your voice down," he whispered. "I came to get you out."

Franklin's jaw dropped.

The familiar expression made Gianni eager to touch him. God, how he'd missed Buffy. "Sorry it took me so long." He fumbled with the key, unlocking the cell. "I had a lot to do."

Franklin looked bewildered. He hadn't moved from his spot. "I thought you hated me. You should hate me."

Gianni flung the door open, grabbed Franklin with both hands, and pulled him up to kiss him quick and hard. "I love you too, you idiot." Another violent kiss. "Now let's get out of here."

"Wait." Franklin kissed him this time, hands squeezing his shoulders tightly, as if making sure this was really happening. "What's your plan?"

Gianni rolled his eyes. "We leave. That's the plan. Hurry."

"The guards?"

"Sleeping. Oswald, too. We don't have much time."

"How many in the house? Right now."

"Two guards and Oswald. It's early. If we hurry, they won't be able to follow us outside, even if they do wake up."

"Got it. We should have weapons, just in case. Is there anything?"

Gianni shrugged; he hadn't thought of that. "We shouldn't need them."

"It'll only take a second." Franklin went to the wooden staircase railing and gave it a swift kick.

The sharp crack wasn't loud, but it wasn't nothing. Gianni hoped it wouldn't carry upstairs.

Franklin grabbed one splintered stake of wood and handed a second to him.

Gianni took it. "Let's go."

"You lead. I'll have your back."

The stake in his hand made Gianni nervous. If it came to a fight, they were dead. Three undead vampires against two mortals was shit for odds.

They ascended the first flight of stairs on silent feet. Creeping slowly around the corner to the second flight, they found the coast clear. Franklin followed on Gianni's heels.

Almost there.

A sound came from above: a creaking floorboard.

Gianni froze and held his breath. When only silence met them, he continued around the last corner on the main floor, with only one set of stairs left until ground level and their exit.

What he saw took the air right out of his lungs.

Oswald blocked their path, standing tall and menacing in spite of his ridiculous orange robe. Hands on his hips, he asked through pursed lips, "What do we have here?"

Gianni reached behind him, keeping Franklin at his back and out of Oswald's range. There was no talking his way out of this one. If he could get Franklin out the door, the slayer could make a run for it.

Oswald pointed to Gianni. "One naughty little vampire earning himself a proper spanking." The accusatory finger moved to Franklin. "And one spurned lover who thought his luck had changed for the better." Oswald tsked low in his throat, staring at Gianni with a scowl. "Did you really think I didn't know?'

"How?" Gianni managed, his heart in his throat. Oswald would kill Franklin just to hurt him. He had to get the slayer to flee.

Oswald laughed, a mean sound with no real mirth. "You aren't nearly as good at this as you think. Running around on your 'shopping trips' coming back with jewelry you don't wear and books you don't read. That, and you tripped the alarm." His sinister smile revealed fangs. "Oh, you didn't know about the alarm? You wouldn't. It's silent and alerts my guards to your comings and goings. I've been waiting for this moment."

"Take me. Let him go," Gianni begged as he pulled the keys to the van from his pocket and handed them back to Franklin. "You can punish me all you want, but leave him out of it." To Franklin, he said, "White cargo van, two blocks northeast."

"Oh, Gianni, stop trying to control things. Leave the deceptions to the master and stick to what you're good at—spreading your legs."

"Don't speak to him like that," Franklin thundered, stepping forward.

Gianni was too stunned to stop him.

"My, my, the spurned lover speaks. Afraid I'll hurt his feelings? Go on, defend him if it makes you feel good, but Gianni knows his place. Don't you, pet?"

Franklin lunged for Oswald, but Gianni was faster, grabbing the slayer by the shoulders and hauling him back.

Oswald's mocking laughter filled the room.

"You have to get out," Gianni commanded, pushing Franklin toward the last flight of stairs.

"No. I won't leave you with him."

"Damnit, Franklin, you have to go. He won't kill me."

Gianni turned back to Oswald. The glee sparkling in the sovereign's eyes filled him with rage. He had to try something. Anything. Gianni leapt at the sovereign, stake in hand, aiming for his heart.

Oswald caught him with only a small step backward, redirecting Gianni's wrist so the stake struck thin air. Gianni was no match for Oswald, but he didn't have to beat him—only delay him long enough for Franklin to run for it. He had a fist in Oswald's hair and yanked with all his might.

As he struggled in Oswald's iron hold, Gianni screamed to Franklin. "You need to go!"

Instead, Franklin leapt into the fray, attacking Oswald while the sovereign was preoccupied.

Oswald twisted from Gianni's hold and blocked Franklin's strike with ease. He swung the smaller vampire behind him and squared off against the slayer.

Gianni jumped onto Oswald's back and clung there. "Franklin, go! He won't kill me."

Oswald roared and reared backward, slamming Gianni against the wall with such force the air was knocked from his lungs. Gianni lost his grip and sank to the floor, leaving Oswald free to go after Franklin.

Gianni coughed and sputtered, a crimson foam on his lips. It couldn't have been much worse—until it was.

Two guards sauntered into the room.

BAD ODDS

Franklin

"Need some help, boss?" the smaller of the guards asked, as if offering to put away groceries instead of taking out a rampaging slayer.

Good, let them underestimate me, thought Franklin. Slaying vampires was his job.

"I want them alive," Oswald said, unfazed.

Gianni was on the ground holding his chest but otherwise seemed okay. Franklin would not abandon him. He eyed the old vampire as the guards, Bigs and Smalls, crept forward. If Gianni could keep Oswald distracted, he could take them out.

He dodged a blow from Oswald, quick on his feet and a stronger opponent than the vampire had expected. Franklin ducked past him and signaled to Gianni, pointing a thumb at Oswald. Gianni gave a short nod.

Bigs lumbered straight for him while Smalls held back, observing. While captive, Franklin had had time to analyze the guards' movements and pick apart their personalities. Bigs resented having to care for a prisoner, especially a human slayer. He would be overconfident and eager for the chance to take on Franklin.

Franklin came at Bigs with a telegraphed uppercut, leaving his side wide open. Bigs took the bait, going for an easy punch to the ribs. Franklin spun, ducked, and took out his legs with a round kick.

Bigs was down!

Franklin risked a quick glance backward. Gianni was pinned to the wall by his throat.

Smalls watched Gianni struggle, grinning and not paying attention to Franklin.

Bigs tried to clamber back to his feet, but a swift knee to the chin sent him sprawling. Franklin plunged the stake through the vampire's heart and pulled it out again, dripping with blood. Bigs died with a loud grunt.

One down.

Smalls rounded on him.

Smalls would be tougher. Franklin guessed they shared a similar fighting style, quick and clean. One mistake, and Smalls would have him. Franklin rolled his shoulders, keeping loose as the smaller guard began to close in.

Gianni was squealing, but Franklin had to trust him. He'd said Oswald wouldn't kill him; he'd better be right.

The guard struck past his defense, direct to Franklin's kidneys.

Pain spiked. Franklin used it to channel his focus. He slashed out with the stake but missed his target, slicing a gash across the collarbone instead of into the vampire's heart.

First blood to Franklin.

After two weeks in a cage, he itched for this fight. He'd lost some muscle mass and, with it, some power, but his speed and agility weren't affected.

With a yell, Franklin darted forward, throwing a punch.

Smalls blocked, but Franklin anticipated it, stepping forward and kneeing the vampire in the groin.

Smalls was stunned long enough to leave himself open.

Bones crunched as Franklin slammed the stake brutally through the heart.

Two down.

One to go.

Franklin spun. His lover was pinned against a wall, crying out in anguish.

Oswald's back was turned, and Franklin went for the kill, aiming the stake to pierce the heart from behind.

So fast Franklin could hardly see it, the older vampire turned, caught Franklin's wrist, and squeezed, forcing his hand open. The stake fell.

Behind him, Gianni sank to the floor.

Shit.

Wrist trapped in place, he used Oswald's hold as a counter-balance to kick. The vampire dodged and bent Franklin in half with a tug, landing a savage blow to Franklin's lower back.

Franklin dropped to his hands and knees, gasping. He braced himself, muscles rigid, anticipating a blow that did not come. Lifting his head and rising back to his feet, he only had a second to regroup.

Oswald had taken hold of Gianni by his biceps.

Franklin took a running leap and plowed into Oswald's side. The sovereign crashed into an end table with such force the top split in two with a loud crack.

Franklin grabbed Gianni by the waist. "Run!" He pushed Gianni toward the staircase and dashed after him. Maybe they could get outside. They sped up the last flight to the ground floor.

Oswald followed in a flash of movement—impossibly fast, dashing Franklin's hope of a quick escape. He flung Franklin to the side, an effortless gesture leaving Franklin crumpled against a window.

Dark. It was dark out already. Even if they did get out, Oswald could follow. Ignoring his pain, Franklin heard Gianni's cries. It was time to end this.

The sovereign twisted Gianni in his grip like a rag doll, clutching him to his chest with a gleaming knife held to the smaller vampire's throat.

"He thinks I won't kill him, but what do you think, slayer?" Oswald asked through bared fangs. "Are you willing to take that risk?"

Gianni's neck bled freely. The brute had bitten him again, and the blade threatened further damage. Despite the injuries, Gianni's eyes blazed with defiance. He stared directly at Franklin.

"He won't kill me." Gianni gave the slightest of nods in Franklin's direction.

Franklin prepared to attack.

Gianni turned bravely into the knife, slashing his own skin and biting ruthlessly through Oswald's wrist.

The larger vampire shouted and dropped the blade as Gianni spit a chunk of his flesh to the ground. Blood gushed from the wound. Gianni had severed a main artery and was grabbing the flailing forearm for another bite.

"Dig the hole deeper, strumpet," Oswald barked. "You'll be sure to regret it."

Franklin surged forward, knocking all three of them to the ground.

Knees on Oswald's chest, Franklin punched the vampire with one hand while digging for his pocket knife with the other. Gianni drank deeply from Oswald's wrist, his mouth covered in red. Blood pooled around them.

Oswald let out a howl and flung them both away from him in opposite directions.

Gianni grabbed the stake from the floor. To give him an opening, Franklin dove for Oswald and plunged the little knife into his eye.

The sovereign lashed out at Franklin, forcing his head to the side and going for his throat.

Even as fangs pierced his flesh, Franklin aimed for the jugular. Maybe Gianni could finish the job.

His throat ached where Oswald's vicious teeth held him in place. The vampire grabbed his stabbing hand and forced it backward. He lost the knife, but the damage had been done.

Oswald was now bleeding from three places.

Gianni was on them in a flash, yelling as he slammed the stake through Oswald's back—but he missed the heart.

Oswald ripped his fangs from Franklin's neck and spun around. "You will pay for your betrayal!" He took Gianni by the neck again, lifting the little vampire off his feet.

Franklin surged for the fallen stake. Movement outside the window caught his eye.

Hunters. A full squadron. Moving in fast.

"The Scourge! They're raiding!" Franklin yelled. He had to get Gianni out.

Gianni's feet dangled in the air. There was no way he could breathe.

It was now or never.

With one last lunge, Franklin landed a fearsome strike while Oswald's attention was on the window. Ribs snapped as Franklin thrust deep, bruising his fist with the impact.

Oswald fell with a high-pitched whine, clutching the stake protruding from his chest. No way to know if it had hit its mark. They had to get out now.

"Gianni..." Oswald cried.

Gianni was on the ground in a heap, staring at the fallen vampire. Franklin scooped his trembling lover into his arms. "Is there another way out? They'll have us surrounded."

Shouts sounded from outside the house. The troops were closing in.

"Back door." Gianni pointed.

Franklin sprinted down a hall and through a dining room, holding Gianni close.

"I can run. Put me down."

Franklin set him on his feet and rushed to unlock the door. "Check the window."

"It's no good—they're in the back too. This way, hurry." Gianni blazed down the hallway back to the stairs.

Oswald lay in an expanding puddle of his own blood.

They tore past him and flew up the stairs just as the Scourge's men kicked in the door.

"You sure about this?" Franklin asked, racing up the stairs behind him.

The troops' footfalls pounded through the house and into the stairwell—down instead of up.

"Oz owns the next house. They're row houses; these two connect." Gianni dashed through a corridor into the neighboring house.

Franklin followed at his heels, down another set of steps to the ground level and a side door.

Gianni flung it open to an alleyway, and they made a break for it.

"You okay?" Franklin asked, flying down the city streets in Gianni's monster of a van. His heart beat wildly, adrenaline pumping through his veins.

Gianni gasped for air in the passenger seat and nodded, his hand clamped over the bleeding bite wounds on his neck. "Are you?"

"Yeah."

"Is he dead?"

"I don't know. I may have missed his heart."

"The Scourge will kill him," Gianni murmured.

Probably. Or maybe they'd take him prisoner. "We need to pull over somewhere and check your wounds."

"And yours."

Franklin drove another mile before stopping on the highway entrance ramp. Flashers on, they climbed into the back to patch each other up.

"Come here. Yours are easy. Let me." Gianni tugged him in, and Franklin went. Gianni licked at his throat, long broad swipes, closing the wounds and lapping up the blood from his skin.

"I wish I could do the same for you." Franklin assessed Gianni's wounds. The vampire's neck and chest were covered in blood.

"I'll be all right." Gianni produced a first aid kit. "Clean me off and check to see if the bleeding has stopped."

Franklin used alcohol on a cloth to wipe Gianni's neck and shoulders. His flesh was littered in bite marks and a nasty cut from the silver knife. Oswald's attacks had been savage. Blood still oozed from the wounds but didn't flow.

While Franklin worked, Gianni dug through the kit. He pressed a tube of skin glue into Franklin's hand. "This will help. Hurry, I want to put more distance between us and them."

Franklin covered Gianni's torn skin with the smelly liquid.

"Good enough." Gianni took the tube from him and capped it.

Franklin watched Gianni closely. His movements had become sluggish; his eyes were dull. "You've lost a lot of blood. Will you be okay?"

Gianni locked eyes with Franklin and nodded. "He's left me bleeding for hours before, and I didn't die."

Franklin wanted to stab Oswald all over again.

23

LIKE A DOG

Gianni

hile the van headed west out of Pennsylvania, Gianni sat shivering in the passenger seat. It was probably shock. He took deep breaths and waited for it to pass.

Franklin drove, pointing them toward the mountains of West Virginia where they'd hide out until they healed. One task remained, and as much as he'd rather press on, it needed to happen before they went any farther.

"Franklin…in the basement… Why did you tell me it wasn't safe at Oswald's?"

The slayer took a deep breath before he answered. "You're going to hate this. *I* hate this, but I don't see another way."

"Don't stall, just tell me." Gianni had figured it out on his own, but they had to address it together.

"I have the Scourge's GPS tracking chip—"

"So ditch it."

"—embedded in the back of my neck. I'm going to have to get you to safety, then keep going. It isn't safe for you to be with me. They'll come for us. They want you."

"What the fuck?" The Scourge was seriously on his shit list. "They put a chip in your back like a dog? That didn't ring any alarm bells?"

"It's standard procedure. We all have one."

"You aren't making it sound better. Pull over."

Franklin turned down a side street, an expression of misery on his face. "I'll leave you now if that's what you want, but are you sure you're safe to drive? You look pretty out of it."

"I feel pretty out of it." The van stopped. "I just got you—I'm not giving you up. Get in the back. I'm going to take it out."

Franklin's eyes grew wide. "I'm not sure where it is or how deep." He was already moving out of the driver's seat and crawling into the cargo section.

"I'll find it." Gianni followed him back to the mattress he'd stashed there. "I'll get it out, and whatever damage I cause, I'll heal with my blood. If you can take the pain, it'll be over in a few minutes, and we'll be free of them."

"You're too weak to give me your blood now," Franklin protested. "It's dangerous."

"It's not. I'll be fine. I gorged myself on Oswald's. We have hours before the cravings start. More on that later. I'm strong enough to help you now." Gianni pushed on Franklin's shoulders until he sat, then climbed into position behind him, fingering his neck. "I don't see a scar. Where do you think it is? Your best guess."

Franklin indicated his upper back, to the left of his spine. "Somewhere in there is where it went in, but they can drift. Could be anywhere."

"It'll be there," Gianni said, pressing into the flesh, feeling for anything foreign. No luck. "Take your shirt off."

Franklin peeled the disgusting garment away to reveal the mostly clean skin beneath. Gianni straddled his legs on the outside of Franklin's hips and wrapped an arm around his waist to hold him in place. Leaning in, he licked the area with a broad swipe of his tongue. The mild numbing effect of his saliva would only work on the skin, but Gianni might have to bite deep into muscle. There would be pain.

"You ready?"

"Yeah, do it."

Gianni slipped his fangs into the flesh. Blood pooled in his mouth, and though it was as divine as he remembered, he resolutely ignored the taste. He closed his eyes, feeling for the chip.

Nothing.

Gianni retracted his fangs and ventured in again, slightly further down. This time, Franklin flinched. It would need to be a grid search. One bite at a time.

Gianni's fangs sank in. Still nothing. He pressed deeper. No chip. He released Franklin and licked the blood away. Lower, he bit again.

Franklin whimpered, and his muscles flexed in protest under Gianni's teeth. The longer this went on, the more it would hurt.

Gianni changed tactics. While he angled his fangs, searching for the chip, he also pressed his groin to Franklin's ass and used his grip to pull their bodies tight together. His fingers found Franklin's nipple and teased it to hardness. Gianni retracted his fangs.

"So good for me, baby," he crooned into Franklin's ear, licking the rim. "Just a bit longer." Gianni lapped the blood from the punctures. "Can you take it for me?"

"Jesus," Franklin cursed, his hands gripping Gianni's thighs. "Yeah, I'm okay. Keep going."

Gianni tweaked his other nipple and pressed his teeth firmly in once more.

Franklin moaned.

Gianni probed, but felt only flesh. *Damn.* Franklin's blood dripped down his back. Gianni gathered it on his tongue, swallowed, and tried again.

Nothing.

One hand continued to fondle Franklin's nipple while the other cast downward to palm his dick. At least in this he was confident. He could make it good for Franklin.

"Fuck. Gianni, yes." Franklin was hard and straining against his pants.

"Pull out your cock," Gianni murmured into his ear. "I need it."

While Franklin unfastened his pants, Gianni started again from the top. Franklin didn't react to the bite, too busy freeing his dick for Gianni's hand.

No chip.

He bit again into Franklin's shoulder and stroked the length of him with his hand. Another try. Gianni's teeth parted skin, wet and bloody; Franklin's taste stoked his appetite. Gianni was hard against Franklin's lower back and pressed against him.

His tooth struck something hard and mobile, which definitely felt as though it didn't belong there. Finally!

With a bruising grip on Franklin's dick to distract him, Gianni brought his blunt lower teeth to meet his fangs, cutting through muscle and closing in over the chip. Squeezing tightly, he grasped and yanked it from Franklin's back, fast, like ripping off a Band-Aid.

Franklin gasped, and a wail escaped his throat.

Gianni spat the chip on the floor.

"Sorry, sorry," Gianni soothed. He swiped his thumb over Franklin's slit and gave the head a gentle squeeze. "It's out."

"Thank god. Uh, yeah, like that," Franklin gasped and pushed himself harder into Gianni's hand.

"We should get rid of it."

"Don't stop." Franklin squeezed Gianni's thighs and tipped his head back.

"I won't." Gianni lapped the blood from Franklin's back, closing the wounds while he freed his own cock from its restraint.

"Get your pants down," Gianni ordered.

Franklin braced himself on one arm and tugged his pants over his ass with the other until they were trapped around his thighs. They settled back into place, Gianni's erection trapped firmly between them and pressed against Franklin's lower back.

"Is this okay?"

"Yes," Franklin breathed, voice shaky. "Better than okay."

"Good."

They moved against each other, Franklin fucking Gianni's fist, Gianni working his hips against Franklin's backside, leaking cum between them.

Franklin reached behind to cradle Gianni's head in his hand. He twisted around for a kiss. Their lips met, tongues seeking, Franklin licking his own blood from Gianni's teeth.

Gianni was moaning around Franklin's tongue. Franklin had to drink from him, to be sure the injuries to his back would heal. His skin was littered with bite marks. Gianni broke from the kiss and bit into his own wrist, placing the bleeding wound to Franklin's mouth.

"Drink," he ordered. Franklin obeyed, soft tongue hot against the sensitive skin. Gianni couldn't take it. He was going to come.

"Please," Gianni begged, working Franklin's cock relentlessly. "Together."

"Yes," mumbled Franklin into his wrist, sucking at the bite wound.

They moved at a savage pace, bodies rocking, mouths open on each other's flesh. Gianni shivered with want, his body cascading toward the edge.

"Gonna come," Gianni panted out against Franklin's ear.

They spilled over in waves, thrusting, coming, panting all the way through. Franklin shook with his release, moaning into Gianni's wrist.

Gianni trembled against Franklin's broad back. He had

enough sense to lick the punctures on his wrist closed, then trailed his hands back over Franklin's torso, mapping his pecs and tracing each ab.

"Fuck," Franklin sighed out, leaning further into the embrace.

They came down slowly. Gianni matched his breathing to Franklin's, their chests expanding and contracting in sync.

"That wasn't what I was expecting," Franklin said with a touch of happy laughter in his voice.

"Me neither. It was so much better."

"Yeah."

"You were amazing back there, you know? Fighting for me."

"Never had something so important to fight for."

Gianni kissed Franklin's back where he'd bitten. The skin was pink and thin, but whole.

"How do you feel?" Gianni asked.

"Amazing. Perfect. Good as new. If only your blood could heal you the way it does me."

"If only." Gianni felt good too, but underneath the high, he knew he was beat up. Soon he'd crave Oswald's blood, another conversation he dreaded. He could put it off for a couple of hours. Long enough to get some distance between them and that damned chip.

Gianni squeezed Franklin's thighs with his own. "We need to get going." He inched away.

Franklin sat up on his own, and they shuffled to fasten their pants.

"Where is it?" Franklin asked.

Gianni picked up the bloody chip from the floor and handed it over.

"Smaller than I thought." Franklin turned it in his fingers.

"Let's get rid of it."

"I'll put it under the tire. With any luck, that will destroy the signal."

"Do that. Then we should both change into fresh clothes. I bought things for you."

"Thank you." Franklin opened the sliding door to ditch the chip while Gianni grabbed a duffel bag. He chose outfits for each of them and began to strip off the dirty things. Blood caked on his shirt, sticky and cold. It was a relief to peel off. Franklin did the same.

"That beard is hot on you."

"Is it?"

"Mm, yes. Makes me want to call you *daddy*." Gianni winked.

Franklin flushed. "Maybe I'll keep it."

Franklin

The drive to a campground in the mountains of West Virginia would take four hours. Franklin had a lot of questions, but Gianni looked tired. After exchanging texts with Hayleigh, a stillness overcame the vampire, and he stared at the passing scenery in a daze.

"You can lie down in the back if you want," Franklin offered. "I'll wake you when we get there."

Gianni's head rolled lazily toward him, a closed-lip smile on his face. "Thanks, but I want to be with you. I'll be all right."

Silence drifted between them as Franklin gathered his thoughts. The white noise of the motor combined with the dissipating adrenaline soothed his nerves. The modicum of safety they'd carved out for themselves provided the mental space for Franklin to think. With so much to say, it was impossible to know where to start. He owed Gianni the apology of a lifetime, but this didn't seem the moment.

"What's going to happen now?" Franklin asked.

Gianni huffed. "That's a loaded question."

Franklin glanced at him from the corner of his eye. Gianni was staring forward. He looked smaller when he was overwhelmed.

The silence stretched for so long, Franklin thought Gianni wouldn't answer, but then his weary voice carried over the road noise. "Did you mean what happens when we get to West Virginia or what happens after? Because my plans only extended so far."

"Don't worry about it," Franklin said. "We'll be all right. I'll take care of you."

"I just might let you."

The interstate was dark through this section of rolling hills. Amish country. Franklin felt better the farther they got from the city.

"With any luck," Gianni's voice stirred the silence, "they'll think I'm dead—the Vampire Council. I don't know about you, but I've committed a capital offense. Attacking a sovereign means a death sentence."

"I attacked him. You're innocent." Franklin hadn't yet considered the legal ramifications of what they'd done. He'd been so certain the Scourge would capture him, he'd given up on that line of thinking. But what of Gianni? The vampire was already isolated in his society. What would happen now? "In any case, it was self-defense."

"I don't think the Council will see it that way. I didn't stop you. I helped." Gianni swiveled in his seat to face him. "I sided with a slayer against a fellow vampire."

"Nobody needs to know that."

"We're still fugitives."

"I'm sorry." Franklin's heart was sinking as the implications set in. "I've taken everything from you."

"What? No." Gianni reached across the divide and rested his hand on Franklin's thigh. His tone was serious. "I never had anything before I found you. Not really." He gave Franklin's leg a squeeze. "All that shit I said to you in the basement—I was mad, and it spewed out of me like vomit. I didn't mean any of it, okay? I felt bad as soon as I'd said it."

Franklin shook his head. "No, you were right. Everything you said. But I swear, I wasn't going to let them take you. I planned on telling you all of it. I was going to warn you to leave and stay away. I thought we had more time, and then poof. It was too late. This is all my fault."

Was Gianni actually laughing? Franklin was pouring his heart out, and the vampire was giggling.

"You're so dumb sometimes," Gianni said through a smile. "I actually imagined you apologizing for this, you know. But in my imagination we were somber. Now, it's happening, and we're in a literal van fort, and I'm not even mad anymore."

"I really am sorry," Franklin mumbled.

"I know. It's okay."

"Um, so…does this mean you forgive me?"

"It's going to be hard to trust you." Gianni's laughter died away. "I'm not saying that to make you feel bad, but after everything I let Oswald do to me, and then you…" Gianni was talking with his hands now, waving them at the windshield. "You may not have meant to hurt me, but that's what happened. Then I had to deal with Oswald all over again." Gianni sighed. "I feel run over. I forgive you, but trust is going to take time."

"I understand. I'll do anything." Franklin had never been more sincere in his life.

"That's good to hear because you're going to have to. We need to talk about detox."

"Detox?"

"I've been drinking Oswald's blood. I'm addicted."

This was Franklin's fault. Gianni would suffer—again—for his mistakes. Franklin would spend the rest of his life trying to make up for it.

"I've got you."

24

DETOX

Gianni

The campground featured secluded sites nestled deep in the trees. They arrived in the early morning and picked up a map from the after-hours check-in folder on the office door. Passing a small pond, the bathroom facilities, and a number of camper homes, they took the van to the spot furthest out. Gravel gave way to dirt. Pine trees surrounded the clearing on three sides. Shady all day, perfect if you were a vampire stuck in a van.

Cicadas sung a welcoming chorus. Normally, Gianni would like that sort of thing, but it barely registered over the agitation setting in.

First he would feel jittery. Then cold chills would claim him. When he didn't get the blood his body craved, the pain would start. Would it last a few days? A week? He focused on deep breathing and tried to ignore it.

Gianni both dreaded the thought of Franklin seeing him sick and was relieved not to be alone.

Franklin was investigating the little bedroom. A mattress fit snug between the wheel wells, decorated with soft blankets, pillows, and a down comforter, all in shades of green. Duffel bags lining the side were filled with clothes, food, toiletries, and books. Fabric draped the industrial interior, and a blackout curtain was installed behind the seats to keep out the daylight.

"You've been busy." Franklin took two packs of crackers from the food bag and handed one to Gianni. "I can't believe you did all this."

Gianni took the crackers. He needed to eat, though the thought turned his stomach. "It took longer than I wanted. I had to leave you down there while I went shopping."

"You did what you had to. It's perfect. You thought of everything." Franklin held up a bottle of conditioner, brow raised, then set it back down with the matching bottle of shampoo.

"No need for our hair to dry out just because we're on the lam." Gianni managed a half smile.

"No, can't have that." Franklin shoved a cracker in his mouth and gathered the toiletries. "I haven't had a real shower in weeks. Would you like to join me?"

"I would, but..." Gianni hated to admit weakness, but he'd have to trust Franklin. "I'm already starting to feel sick. I'd better stay here."

"Do you want me to stay?"

"I'll be fine. I need to call Hayleigh anyway. You go. Enjoy."

"I'll be quick."

Alone with nothing but the sound of the wind in the trees and the mating call of bugs, Gianni curled up under a blanket. He'd promised to fill Hayleigh in when they got to safety.

She answered right away. "Did you make it to your hideout?"

"Safe and sound," he confirmed, glad to hear a friend's voice.

"Thank god. How are you feeling?"

"It's starting." Gianni took a deep breath and sighed. "I'm nervous. What if we're not ready for this?"

"You told Franklin about it, though? How did he react? Wait, is he with you?"

"He's showering. I'm alone. He feels terrible. He thinks everything's his fault."

"Everything *is* his fault."

Gianni chuckled. His stomach protested. "He'll take care of me. I know he'll help as much as he can, but there isn't much for him to do. It's just going to take time."

"You could bond with him," she said, direct, as was her style, and one of the reasons Gianni liked her. "That would help."

"And go from one addiction straight to the next? I don't know."

"I can't believe I'm about to say this. After what he did to you—"

"He didn't hurt me on purpose."

"Nevertheless. Listen, you love him. That glimpse I got from your mind made it crystal clear. You've risked everything to save him. Why wouldn't you want to bond with him?"

"I do..." Gianni trailed off. There hadn't been much time to give the option any thought. The idea was appealing.

"Does he love you?"

"He's said as much."

"Do you believe him?"

"Yes." As Gianni said it, he realized it was true.

"Then why suffer when a new bond would help?" Hayleigh prodded.

"Well, when you put it that way..."

"Good. Now, tell me what the hell happened. How'd you get out?"

Gianni gave an edited version of events, which she settled for because he was exhausted. She would let him know when word of the Scourge's raid hit the rumor mill.

Before they hung up, Gianni needed some updates too. "Do you have any news for me? How's Tabea doing on her part?"

"You're going to love this…"

Franklin

Being clean and dressed in fresh clothes felt worlds better. Among the things Gianni had chosen for him were soft linen pants in a faded tan color and a charcoal gray shirt of a knit so fine it felt like silk against his skin. Both fit perfectly, better than his own things. Having a fussy vampire doing his shopping might be nice.

He found Gianni sprawled in a nest of pillows, one phone in his hand and another on his belly. Upon seeing Franklin, he palmed the extra and held it out.

"For you. It's got two numbers, mine and Hayleigh's."

Franklin took it. "You didn't have to do this. Thank you."

"You need a phone." Gianni scooted over to make room for him. "If I'd been thinking straight, I would have bought you a burner, too. As it is, you'll have to wait to call your dad."

"My dad?" He lifted his eyebrows and shook his head. "I'm not going to call my dad." Franklin sat by Gianni's side and closed the door. The interior was lit by a small lamp, casting a soft glow along Gianni's elegant form. He longed to reach out and touch him but wasn't certain if the gesture would be welcomed.

"Won't he be worried about you?" Gianni casually ran his fingers along Franklin's calf. It was so simple for him. Gianni touched and flirted like it was second nature.

"I'm sure he thinks I'm dead. Finding out I'm not would be bad news. Better off staying dead."

"I'm sorry." The fingers stopped at his knee and gave a comforting squeeze.

"Don't be. We never had a good relationship. It's for the best."

"His loss."

"He'd never accept this." Franklin motioned between the two of them.

Gianni smiled and opened his arms. "Then let's make it worth it."

Franklin went to him, hovering over his chest as Gianni's arms closed around him. The vampire tugged until Franklin settled against him and placed kisses along his jawline.

Gianni grabbed his head and redirected his lips where he wanted them. Kissing Gianni was a whole body experience. Warmth spread from their joined mouths all the way to his toes. Gianni's clever tongue was everywhere at once, running along his teeth, caressing his lips. Franklin sucked it into his mouth to savor, making the vampire moan. All traces of doubt slipped away.

When they came up for air, Franklin gazed down to admire lips puffy from kissing, but what he saw were Gianni's eyes shut tight.

"Are you okay?"

Gianni's lids fluttered open to reveal watery hazel eyes. "I'm sorry. I want to be with you, but it's starting. It hurts."

Franklin cupped his cheek. "Hey, no. Don't apologize. What can I do?"

"The sun will be up soon, and I can sleep it off. Tomorrow night will be worse. Could you hold me? Unless…"

Franklin readjusted, settling in against Gianni's side and pulling him close. "Unless what?"

Gianni took a breath, his voice quiet. "Could I drink from you? Just a little? I think it would help. But—"

"Of course. As much as you need."

"You didn't let me finish. If I drink from you regularly, and if you drink from me, the same thing will happen for us as it did with me and Oswald. A blood bond. It's not easy to quit. You have to be sure."

Franklin didn't have to think. "I'm sure."

When Gianni made no move to take him up on it, Franklin placed his fingertips on his chin and turned him so they faced each other.

"Gianni, I'm sure. I'd want it even if it didn't help with the detox, and I especially want to do it knowing it could provide relief." Franklin kissed him. "Please."

"Yes," Gianni whispered and rolled toward him, chest to chest. They tangled their legs together. "Thank you."

Franklin tilted his head back, making room and offering his neck. It was worth everything they'd gone through to get to this point. Wet heat lapped at his throat, drawing a sigh from Franklin's lips. He moved against Gianni's body just to feel all the places they connected, the sensations stronger because of the luxurious fabrics Gianni favored. A sultry warmth burned between them, spiking as fangs slid deep into his flesh. Exquisite.

Franklin's hands spanned the width of Gianni's ribcage, rising and falling with each breath. Feeding him was euphoric pleasure, singular in its ferocity. His cock hardened and pressed into Gianni's abdomen. The vampire began to undulate against him in a sinuous, teasing motion.

Too soon it was over—teeth receded and replaced with that clever tongue, then pursed lips and slick kisses. The motion of their bodies never ceased, Franklin's length trapped tight between them.

Gianni pushed him onto his back and reached into his pants.

Franklin was desperate, but even as Gianni's nimble fingers curled around his cock, he said, "You don't have to."

Gianni knelt over him, caught his gaze, and lowered his mouth until it hovered teasingly over the leaking head. He stopped before making contact.

"What don't I have to do?"

Franklin was beyond words, but the devilish grin on Gianni's face told him to play along. "Get me off. You don't have to."

The tip of Gianni's pink tongue gathered moisture from the slit and then retreated. "Hmm. Good to know. And if I want to?"

Coherent thought grew more intangible by the second. "Oh god. Um. That would be great."

Gianni's lips closed over the head, and his tongue traced the ridge. He placed a kiss on the tip.

"Ask me to." Gianni's eye glittered with raw delight.

Franklin played along. "Please?"

"Please, what?"

"Please, suck my dick," Franklin tried, quivering in Gianni's grasp.

"So polite."

Gianni rewarded him by taking his entire length into his throat in one go. "Jesus!"

Pulling off, Gianni squeezed his cock at the base. "Naughty. That's not my name. Try again."

"Gianni," Franklin groaned, cheeks flushed.

The vampire's grin returned. His hand slid from root to tip, thumb teasing his frenulum. "Full sentences. You can do it. Ask me. Use my name."

"Please, Gianni, suck my dick." Franklin's head thrust back against the pillow. He'd never used words as foreplay.

Tight, wet heat surrounded his cock. Gianni worked him expertly. It would be over in seconds, the vivid, all-consuming passion Gianni's full attention provoked. The vampire gave him no break, no lull to catch his breath. He pulled Franklin's orgasm from him violently, brutal in his love. Franklin shook with it, giving it up, coming down his throat with a guttural howl.

After, as Franklin lay gasping, Gianni crawled up his body and settled against his chest. Franklin wrapped both arms around him while he caught his breath. They were both still fully clothed. Franklin slipped a hand under Gianni's shirt to caress the skin on his lower back.

"That was intense. How'd you get so good?" Franklin asked.

Gianni chuckled, fingers trailing lightly over his nipple. "Don't ruin it by asking questions you don't want the answers to."

Oh.

Franklin was so stupid sometimes. "Sorry, I just…"

Gianni was fully laughing now. "You are the only person who could ask a question like that so innocently. I like that about you. That and the color your face turns when I make you say *dick*." Gianni found his nipple with his teeth and bit it gently through his shirt.

"I like how bossy you are in bed. So hot. It's your turn. What do you want?"

Gianni snuggled deeper into his embrace. "Hold me."

"You sure?" He felt Gianni nod against him. "How are you feeling?"

"Tired, but better. The blood helped. It doesn't hurt so much."

"Good."

Franklin rubbed soothing circles over Gianni's back, up to his shoulders, down to the curve of his cheeks. Before long, the rhythm of his breathing evened out, and Gianni slept. Franklin kissed his hair and continued the gentle massage until sleep claimed him too.

Gianni

When the sun set, Gianni woke curled against Franklin. The

pain wasn't any worse—a dull ache. He wanted blood, but it wasn't Oswald's he craved.

And Franklin's…was available.

"Good evening," Gianni mumbled directly into Franklin's neck. "May I?"

Franklin tipped his head. "You don't have to ask."

Gianni sank his teeth into the inviting flesh and sucked, eager to satiate his thirst. Franklin's blood was decadent and sweet, filling his mouth and coating his throat with heat.

Hot hands gripped his waist, holding him in place, but Gianni had no plans to leave. Not now that they finally had each other. Fantasies of endless nights spent together played out in his mind.

The blood always made him feel that way, carefree and light. But as he withdrew his fangs and closed the wounds, reality set in. They were hiding out in a van, and if anyone knew they were alive, death sentences awaited. They needed to disappear.

"You okay?" Franklin interrupted his train of thought.

Gianni took a moment to assess his body. Maybe a little jittery, with an ache in his bones that was unpleasant but bearable. Surprisingly, that was it. "I was expecting it to be worse."

Franklin squeezed him. "But you're okay?"

"Yes."

"I'm glad."

"I booked this place for a week. I thought I'd need it. This is better. We'll have time to decide what to do next." Gianni shifted in Franklin's hold, kissed his lips, and sat up, a true test of how his stomach was holding up. When the urge to vomit didn't set in, he counted that as a win.

"I need to shower." Gianni pointed to the little cooler on the floor and the camp stove balanced on top. "You must be starving. You can start breakfast. There are eggs and potatoes if you feel like cooking or bagels if you don't. Help yourself."

"What do you want?"

Gianni smiled. "A hot breakfast would be nice, if you don't mind cooking."

"I don't mind."

"Thank you. A small portion for me—my stomach is still a little iffy."

It was just past seven o'clock, and other campers were out. Gianni watched with interest. A family with small children kicking a soccer ball; teenagers milling around a barbecue; an older couple rocking in lawn chairs. Peaceful. So unlike anything else in Gianni's life.

A longing arose, fully formed and vivid. Would Franklin want something like this? A small cabin in a rural setting, surrounded by nature and the scent of evergreens. Gianni could picture them there.

During his shower, the fantasy continued, now including a captivating scenario where Franklin had to chop wood. His broad shoulders would be splendid covered in blue checked flannel. As the water warmed Gianni's body, the image of a simpler life warmed his soul. He took his time washing and peered at the mirror while he toweled dry.

He looked like himself, which was to say he wasn't gaunt or ashen like the last time he'd detoxed. There were no dark circles under his eyes. His skin was vibrant, his vessels bolstered with Franklin's blood, healthy and fresh. Marvelous. The cure for Oswald's damning ownership was Franklin's freely given generosity.

Everything would be different now.

The savory smell wafting from their campsite made his stomach rumble. Perhaps he'd have an appetite after all. Franklin was browning potatoes and had eggs ready for the frying pan. The sight of him at the picnic table tending to the little stove added to the sense of wellbeing that had taken root in his gut.

The night felt like a vacation and passed swiftly as good

times often do. After they'd eaten, Franklin dragged the mattress out of the van, and they curled up together under the stars. The moon was nearly full, casting light across Franklin's handsome features. The sounds of the forest were the perfect accompaniment to their easy conversation.

"I love being in the woods like this," said Franklin, "far from the city."

"It's peaceful. We haven't had much of that lately."

"I'm not sure we've ever had it."

Gianni listened to their breathing, syncing his to Franklin's.

"We have a second chance." Franklin ran his fingers through Gianni's hair. "Maybe we could go somewhere similar? Up north? Canada. A place to lay low. I could get a job, something to get by—"

"Yes," Gianni interrupted. "I mean, really? You'd be okay living in the woods somewhere, because I was thinking—"

"—I've always wanted to get out of the city," Franklin said, matching his excitement.

"Great."

"But it would be okay for you? I mean, you're used to—"

"Fuck what I'm used to."

Franklin laughed. Then his expression turned serious. "What happens when you decide you want to be…turned?"

"I don't know. Is that a deal breaker? What if I want to turn you, too?" At Franklin's blank stare, Gianni continued, "Could we maybe ignore this topic a little longer? We've dealt with so much."

Franklin nodded. "Nothing's a deal breaker, okay?"

"Thanks." Gianni took a breath in relief. He wanted to be turned, only he wasn't in a hurry anymore. Plus, Franklin would look hot with fangs. "And anyway, you don't need to get a job."

"I don't?"

"I have money. I moved it before our escape. It's untraceable."

"I can't let you pay for everything. I have to contribute."

The mental image of Franklin chopping wood for them came back, but this time, he wasn't wearing a shirt at all.

"I can think of a few ways."

———

Franklin

Gianni had produced a laptop, insisting Franklin see an episode of Buffy the Vampire Slayer. It was campy and more than a little silly, but it made Gianni happy.

"Now I see why you called the dog Spike," Franklin said. "I wonder how she's doing."

"Me too." Gianni smiled. "What do you want to watch?"

Franklin hadn't seen much TV, but he remembered nature documentaries narrated by David Attenborough.

"Perfect," Gianni agreed. They relaxed to the gentle voice teaching them about flamingo parades and the trials and tribulations of the dung beetle.

When the jitters got painful, Franklin rubbed Gianni's scalp and pet his hair, soothing the worst of the symptoms which, the vampire assured him, were never all that bad.

"Oswald did this on purpose, didn't he? So you couldn't leave."

Gianni nodded. "Exactly."

"He would come down to the basement to brag." Franklin shook his head. "The things he said about you. Like he owned you, like some sort of trinket he could display."

"Mmhmm, yes. That's how he saw me."

"Did you sleep with him?" The question came out before his brain could stop it.

Gianni stiffened. "Of course I did."

"No, I don't mean did you ever sleep with him." Franklin's

mouth continued without checking in with his filter. "I meant while I was locked up. He said you did."

Gianni eyed him warily. "You ask like you're not ready to hear the answer. Also, it really isn't your business."

That was answer enough. Franklin shouldn't have asked. Not because he blamed Gianni, but because he'd made the vampire uncomfortable.

"What does it matter if I slept with him?" Gianni sounded defensive now.

"It doesn't."

"Don't lie."

"I'm sorry. You're right—it's none of my business." The thought of Gianni sleeping with Oswald because there was no other way out sickened him. Whatever Gianni had done, he'd done it for Franklin.

"I'm an ass," Franklin said. "I don't know why I brought it up."

Neither of them said anything. Gianni snuggled into his chest, and Franklin stroked his back. The silence stretched. Franklin thought Gianni might have fallen asleep, until his voice rose, quiet and a bit muffled.

"I slept with him," Gianni said into Franklin's chest, hiding his face.

"I know."

"I had to."

"I know that, too."

"You're not mad?" Gianni lifted his face to catch Franklin's eyes, vulnerability showing though the murky hazel.

"No way." Franklin met his gaze. "You risked everything to save my life. I'm grateful."

"Yeah, well, you lost everything to save mine, so I guess we're even."

Franklin wasn't sure they'd ever be even, but it was sweet of Gianni to say it.

25

SLOW

Franklin

They began working on their exit strategy, agreeing to flee the country for Quebec, north of Montreal, and rent a cottage. Gianni insisted they swing through Bristol Springs to say goodbye to Hayleigh and Tabea. Franklin thought it was an unnecessary risk but wasn't about to start arguing over something Gianni swore was important. The women would meet them outside of town, and then they'd be off.

It was nearly dawn on their last night in West Virginia. Franklin pulled pajamas from his duffel and sat down to change. Gianni stripped off his own clothes but made no move to retrieve his pajamas. He lay back on their bed, hands beneath his head, and watched Franklin through half-lidded eyes.

Franklin couldn't believe his luck, that this beautiful, lithe body was spread out before him. Not only could he look his fill, he was encouraged to touch. "Do you have any idea how attractive you are?"

Gianni grinned. "I might have some idea, but I like it when you remind me."

Franklin discarded his clothes and stretched out next to him, running his palm from thigh to clavicle in one long, delicious swoop.

"What would you like? I am at your service," Franklin offered, teasing a nipple to hardness with the tip of one finger.

Gianni shivered. "More of that."

Franklin played with the nub, rolling it gently between thumb and forefinger, watching the man beneath him squirm. He leaned in and worked the other one with his tongue. When he let his teeth graze the raised flesh, he was surprised by a resounding smack on his ass.

Gianni had spanked him. "No teeth. Slow and gentle," the vampire ordered. "Don't stop."

That tone of voice did things to Franklin. He could manage slow and gentle. Anything for Gianni. He licked his fingers to wet the other nipple and slid them in circles ever so lightly. With his tongue, he did the same to the other side.

Gianni pushed his chest further into Franklin's mouth. "Yes. That's good." His hands closed over Franklin's shoulders, rubbing circles on his back like the ones Franklin made on his nipples. Gianni writhed under him, little gasps escaping his mouth and urging Franklin on.

"Oh god, Franklin. I want you to fuck me. Will you fuck me?" Gianni reached for something beside the bed.

"Anything you want. *Any way* you want." Franklin kissed the hard little nub.

"Fuck, yes. Use this." He pressed a tube into Franklin's hand. "I want to do it like this, on my back, so I can watch."

Franklin took the lube with a bit of trepidation. He wanted to make it good. In principle, he knew how this worked, but preparing someone was new. Luckily, his mouthy partner had a penchant for ordering him around.

Franklin settled between Gianni's spread legs and unscrewed the cap. "Talk me through it?"

"With pleasure." Gianni's smirk was downright lascivious.

Before the vampire could get another word in, Franklin leaned forward and balanced on one arm to claim Gianni's lips. He licked a broad stripe up Gianni's neck, then returned to his task. Gianni's cock lay flush and rigid on his abdomen. Franklin took hold of him and began to stroke. Gianni's hips rocked in response.

"Tell me how you like it."

"Put your other hand on my hip. Hold me down."

Franklin did, halting the rocking motion. He milked Gianni's dick, the pink tip shiny and glistening. Gianni was brilliantly proportioned, slim waist leading to narrow hips, muscular lean thighs lying open. His cock was thick in Franklin's grip. He wanted to put his mouth on it, to taste him.

Another first.

Franklin sucked the head into his mouth, smooth as silk against his tongue. No wonder people loved to do this. If Gianni was surprised, he hid it well and with a moan. Franklin pressed further down, taking as much as he could till he nearly gagged and had to retreat. He tried again. With some practice, Gianni would fit into his throat. He was eager to try, but the vampire stopped him with a hand in his hair, pulling him off.

"Very ambitious of you, love," Gianni panted, "but I don't want to come that way. I believe I asked you to fuck me."

"I'll get there." Franklin gave the tip a kiss and sat back on his heels. He slicked his fingers with the lube and trailed them from Gianni's cock, over his balls, and across his perineum.

Gianni squirmed. "Fuck, yes, touch me there."

Franklin's pointer finger found the pucker and traced its soft ridges.

Gianni canted his hips, and Franklin's eyes widened at the view. That Gianni trusted him with this was such a turn-on. Franklin palmed his own cock to take the edge off. He coated

Gianni's hole with lube and watched, mesmerized, as the pucker quivered under his touch.

"More, Franklin," Gianni demanded. "Put your fingers in me."

Franklin pressed into the unbelievably tight channel, wringing soft sounds from Gianni. Impossible his cock would fit there. His finger disappeared inside, taking Franklin's breath along with it.

"Another," ordered his lover.

Franklin wasn't certain two would fit. "Are you sure? I don't want to hurt you."

"You won't. It's good. Please."

The *please* did it. Franklin placed a second finger next to the first and watched as Gianni's body made room. With his other hand he stroked Gianni's length, but Gianni pushed him away.

"You'll make me come. Not yet. Gonna come on your cock." Gianni was grinning.

Franklin glanced up at that wicked, dirty mouth. "You can't just say stuff like that." He was touching his own erection now, heavy and throbbing. He'd never been so ready.

"Can't I?" Gianni bore down on his fingers. "Add a third, Franklin. Fuck me with your fingers so I can take that big, thick cock of yours. Want you in me." Gianni's body writhed. "Please, lover, do it."

"You're killing me." Franklin added a third finger. "The way you talk. What it does to me."

"What's it do to you, baby?"

"Fuck. I'm so hard." Franklin was usually quiet during sex, but the talking was hot. "I need you."

"Take me. I'm ready." Gianni drew his knees back.

For a second, Franklin could only stare. His for the taking. He picked up the lube and slicked himself. Lining them up, he rubbed the head against Gianni's hole.

Franklin caught Gianni's hazel gaze. "Ready?"

Gianni nodded. "Slow, Franklin, I like it slow."

Franklin pressed in, watching as Gianni's body took him, bit by glorious bit, to the root. When his hips met Gianni's ass, he paused, checked in. Gianni's mouth was open and his eyes half lidded, the pleasure on his face undeniable.

"Good?"

"So good," Gianni said, his voice breathy. He reached for Franklin, who lowered to tuck his arms under Gianni's shoulders and hold him tight. When Gianni returned the embrace, he began to move.

Franklin kept the motion slow and languid, Gianni arching with him, legs clamped around his waist. They were touching everywhere, warm and safe and infinitely sensual. Gianni stretched around him where they connected, a hot snug fit sending a thrill straight through to his toes.

"Franklin, touch me," Gianni whispered into his ear, the words followed by his tongue.

Franklin made room between them and took Gianni, throbbing and stiff, in his hand. He worked him in smooth, even strokes, in time with his thrusts. They moved together, slowly stoking the intensity, chasing the same high.

"Gonna come," Gianni moaned against his ear. "Fuck me, Franklin. Come in me."

Gianni spasmed in his hand and around his cock. The tremors gripped him, sent him over the edge. Franklin gave several hard, stuttering thrusts and emptied himself deep inside his lover.

Still shaking, he collapsed against Gianni's chest, the vampire tugging him down and claiming his lips. They panted into each other's mouths, coming down from the euphoria in stages. Slow.

"Fuck," Gianni breathed into his mouth. "So good."

It was too soon for words.

Gianni used his grip on Franklin's hair to tilt his head to the side. Franklin realized what he wanted a second too late to help, but Gianni managed, sinking his fangs into Franklin's throat with a low groan.

The sharp hint of pain sent a shiver down his spine, and his cock spasmed again. Franklin gave a tiny thrust. Gianni matched it with his hips. As the vampire sucked at his neck, Franklin hopelessly drove himself deeper into Gianni's tight heat. Gianni's cock jumped where it was trapped. It was near to a second orgasm, different in intensity, but no less pleasurable. The tremors abated as Gianni licked the flesh closed and withdrew.

"Now you," Gianni said and produced a scalpel from god knew where.

Before Franklin could freak out, the vampire cut a slice into his own neck. The vibrant red blood welling on the pale white skin of Gianni's throat was irresistible. Franklin bent to lap it up. When that was gone, he sucked at the wound for more and was rewarded with another mouthful. He licked at the cut until the blood flow grew sluggish.

Gianni handed him a cloth. "Put pressure on it."

Franklin held the cloth tight against his neck and kissed his ear.

"Holy shit," was all he could manage to say.

"You got that right, *Daddy*," Gianni purred.

"Fuck, so dirty." Franklin felt his cheeks flush.

Gianni grinned beneath him. He pulled Franklin down by the scruff on his cheeks for another kiss. With a groan, he let his legs fall back to the bed.

Franklin slid out of him and off to the side, keeping the vampire tucked in close.

"I love how mouthy you get during sex," Franklin said.

"Only during sex?"

"All of the time."

"That's good because you bring that out in me." Gianni smiled. "Kiss me again."

Franklin did as he was told.

Gianni made everything so effortless.

223

REUNION

Gianni

The drive toward Bristol Springs passed smoothly. Plans for their road trip to Canada were set, an Airbnb in Joliette, Quebec already booked. Only one rendezvous was left before they could go.

Franklin pulled into the rest stop off I-79 as Gianni scanned the area for Hayleigh and Tabea. The women waited for them in the far parking space, leaning side by side against the hood of Tabea's beat-up Honda. They waved as the giant van approached.

"You don't think Tabea is still mad at me, do you?" Franklin asked.

"What? No way. She's not the type to hold a grudge."

"I feel bad about what happened." Franklin parked in the adjacent space.

"So apologize, dummy. She'll forgive you."

Gianni leapt from the van and directly into Hayleigh's arms. He kissed her, then hurriedly turned to Tabea for another hug.

"Thank you for coming," Gianni said against Tabea's cheek,

which he also kissed. They'd come through for him big time, and Franklin was about to find out the extent of all his planning.

Suddenly, Gianni was nervous. This was going to be a big commitment—what if he'd made the wrong call?

The women greeted Franklin, more subdued but no less friendly.

"Hey, I'm sorry about that night at your house. I never meant to scare you," Franklin stumbled out an apology right off the bat. Gianni mentally dubbed him King of Awkward.

"No worries. I guess you got over it." She gestured to Gianni, who'd leaned into Franklin's side and thrown an arm around his waist. Franklin held him loosely. Gianni would never tire of the casual closeness they indulged in.

"You could say that." Franklin grinned.

"Well," said Hayleigh, clapping her hands together, "are you ready for the big surprise?"

The butterflies in Gianni's stomach were line dancing. He hoped Franklin would be happy. "It's now or never. Let's do it."

"What surprise?" Franklin eyed the group curiously.

Tabea opened the back door of the SUV, and out hopped Spike, tongue lolling as she rounded the corner. Recognizing Franklin, her almond-shaped brown eyes lit up, and she tugged at the leash to get to him, Tabea laughing as she trailed behind.

"She remembers you," Hayleigh said with a grin.

"Spike!" Franklin knelt as the dog rushed over, reaching for her shoulders and giving her a rub. He scratched behind the dog's ears as she covered his face in kisses.

"Hey girl, good girl…how've you been?" He kissed her back, right on the snout.

Relief washed over Gianni at the heartwarming reunion. He'd been pretty sure Franklin would want Spike, but seeing it play out in front of him was marvelous.

He stood next to Hayleigh and gave her a nudge. "Any news? From the raid?"

She nodded, eyes shining. "You're in the clear. The Vampire Council thinks the Scourge is to blame for the deaths of the guards. They don't know what's become of you. You're presumed missing or dead."

It was too soon for a sigh of relief. "And…Oswald?"

"Missing. Surely they killed him."

"Surely." Oswald had to be dead. They'd seen him fall, stake embedded in his chest. The Scourge must have taken his body. Gianni wouldn't dwell on it, not when he was free to disappear with Franklin.

Hayleigh took his elbow. "If you need someone to turn you, I'm not powerful like a sovereign, but I'd do it. You know that, right?"

Gianni nodded, overwhelmed. "Thank you. I won't forget." He kissed her and took a deep breath. That bridge he'd cross another night.

Gianni knelt next to Franklin to say hello to Spike. She sniffed his hand and allowed herself to be petted before giving Gianni a lick, then turned her attention back to Franklin.

"I can't believe you did this." Franklin's eyes shone with pleasure. He kissed Gianni quick and hard, then focused on the women. "All of you! I can't believe you did this. Thank you."

"I've had her for a week now," Tabea said. "She's a great dog, housebroken and polite. She even knows a few tricks."

"Wow." Franklin took the leash. "Show me?"

"Sure, but she doesn't work for free. Gianni, come help me with her things, and we'll get some treats."

Gianni rounded the Honda with her to collect Spike's food and toys.

Tabea stopped him with a hand on his elbow. "Thank you for paying off my tuition. You have no idea how much of a burden you took off my shoulders."

"You're welcome." They indulged in another warm hug. "It was a good trade, yes? Thank you for rescuing my dog."

"You mean his dog?" she said with a broad smile.

"Yeah, but I'm confident I can bribe her into liking me too. She's a pushover for turkey."

"She loves these too. Come on." Tabea handed Gianni some treats, and they rejoined the group. "Gianni, get her attention and ask her to sit."

Franklin and the dog were still canoodling cheerfully, but she turned her head when Gianni called. He showed her the treat, and she perked up.

"Spike, sit," Gianni requested.

Voila. Butt on the ground. "Good girl!" Gianni gave her a treat. Spike was officially the best dog ever.

"Now try *down* and *bang*," Tabea suggested.

"Spike, down," Gianni said, and the dog lay down. He tossed her another treat. "Good girl. Spike, bang." She rolled to her side and played dead, one floppy brown ear splayed open. Gianni laughed and gave her the rest of the handful.

"She's so smart," Franklin said to Tabea. "You've been busy."

"She's a quick learner." Tabea gave Spike an affectionate scratch behind her fuzzy ear. "It was actually really fun. Now I want a dog, damn it."

They laughed together. Gianni was sad to be leaving them. These women were kind and had been there when he'd needed a friend, and he didn't know when he'd see them again. He turned to Hayleigh.

"Thanks for everything. I'm going to miss you."

She hugged him tightly. "I'll miss you too." Then, to Franklin, "You'll take good care of him?"

Franklin nodded sincerely. "I promise."

Gianni gave Tabea a final embrace. "Thank you. You have my number if you ever need anything. Keep in touch."

She nodded against his shoulder. "You bet."

Franklin loaded the dog and all of her things into their van and climbed into the driver's seat.

Gianni waved goodbye until he couldn't see the two women anymore.

"That was a rollercoaster." Gianni breathed a contented sigh. "Nervous, happy, sad. I'm exhausted."

"I cannot believe you got us a dog," Franklin said, happiness shining through in his voice. "I've always wanted a dog!"

Gianni chuckled. "I know."

"You are the best vampire boyfriend in the world."

"I had better be the only one."

"The only one," Franklin corrected. "And also the best."

Gianni's laughter filled the van.

The End

AUTHOR'S NOTE

Two novels written years apart and with several books between them are now scheduled to release back to back. If you read both, please note the author is obsessed with the concept of a vampire born alive with a beating heart and human weaknesses. That idea is explored in similar but different ways in each novel. Don't expect the rules in *Slay My Love* to apply to *Forbidden Bond* and vice versa. If you enjoy the concept as much as Lee does, stay tuned because she has a third idea brewing.

ABOUT THE AUTHOR

Lee Colgin has loved vampires since she read *Dracula* on a hot sunny beach at 13 years old. She lives in North Carolina with lots of dogs and her husband. No, he's not a vampire, but she loves him anyway. Lee likes to work out so she can eat the maximum amount of cookies with her pizza. Ask her how much she can bench press.

Connect with Lee
Email: LeeColgin@gmail.com
Facebook: www.facebook.com/groups/leecolgin
Twitter: www.twitter.com/leecolgin
Website: www.leecolgin.com
Newsletter: http://eepurl.com/gJEu35

www.ingramcontent.com/pod-product-compliance
Lightning Source LLC
Chambersburg PA
CBHW021320190726
48288CB00003B/896